T0368380

FREEDOM VOYAGE

Sylvia Robbins

authorHOUSE®

AuthorHouse™
1663 Liberty Drive
Bloomington, IN 47403
www.authorhouse.com
Phone: 833-262-8899

*All names have been changed to protect the innocent and the guilty.
The events depicted may or may not have occurred.*

Published by AuthorHouse 03/12/2025

ISBN: 979-8-8230-4510-0 (sc)
ISBN: 979-8-8230-4511-7 (e)

Library of Congress Control Number: 2025904721

Print information available on the last page.

Dedicated to Craig, my travel companion and friend.
And to all my fellow world travelers for
sharing the journey of a lifetime.

CONTENTS

Adventure of a Lifetime

A FTER hearing the words "around the world cruise," I was hooked. I immediately started researching and saving for the trip of a lifetime. I never expected my six-month world cruise to be full of trauma and drama on the high seas. I never could have predicted what would happen and how I would be involved. Looking back to the winter and spring of 2024, I am still moved in many ways.

My name is Raven Woodley, and as I write this, I have endured a milestone and had my seventieth birthday. I am all about ease and comfort. My hair is grey and I keep it short so the natural curl is evident. A quick towel dry and a brush are all I need to get ready in the morning. No make-up is necessary. I wore business suits during my career so I never want to wear one again. Throw on drawstring black or navy pants and a colorful cotton top, and I am out the door. I am more of a couch potato than an athlete and had a desk job. I have worked at or thought about getting thinner for most of my life. I have lost the same twenty pounds countless times.

I was born with an innate need for order and organization, which took me on a varied career path until I landed a project management position for information technology services in the healthcare sector. In that high-stress environment, I needed several vacations a year to escape it all and cruising perfectly fit that need. I have been privileged to travel to more than sixty countries. I worked hard so I could travel the world. Many countries I visited were onboard a cruise ship, unpacked once, and no long flights were needed. It is my favorite way to see new and exciting places and rejuvenate. I try hard to live my life with the least amount of drama. Cruising to me is a Calgon bath on steroids.

I first heard about the concept of a world cruise in 1978, and honestly, it is so long ago that I do not know how I came to know about such a thing. However, I was fascinated and intrigued way back then. You would expect that once all the saving and scrimping had been done and retirement had been taken, setting sail would be a breeze, but that was not to be.

CHAPTER 1

Decisions, Decisions, Decisions

AFTER retiring, downsizing, and adjusting to these massive life changes, I was finally ready to book a world cruise and have my big adventure as a solo traveler. I was raised by a fiercely independent woman and have traveled solo to foreign destinations. I knew this decision would double my cruise fare and influence my chosen cruise line. Still, I was uncomfortable finding a cabin mate I did not know and living with them in a one-hundred-sixty-square-foot room for four months or more.

Only a handful of cruise lines circumnavigate the globe, and each of them does only one around the world cruise a year. Most of them leave in January and go west. Going west gets you lots of extra sleep, which has always been my preference. Cruise lines generally include African or Middle Eastern ports, not both. I have always preferred Africa since I am all about seeing wildlife in its natural habitat. Safaris are my happy place.

After I had booked and canceled a few world cruise options due to different itineraries, I received a world cruise brochure from a small ship luxury brand called SeaSpirit, and literally, my jaw dropped. Not only because the pamphlet was exquisitely done, but the itinerary was perfect, for one hundred and eighty days, a full six months. Typically, world cruises are for about four or five months. It was more expensive but included wi-fi, gratuities, medical services, laundry, and non-alcoholic beverages. It also included many shore excursions, a pre-hotel stay, airport transfers, luggage shipping, and spa treatments. On most other cruise lines, there would be additional charges for each of these, and I would have received a hefty bill when I disembarked the ship. I appreciated the idea of not thinking about the cost whenever I asked for a soda or sent my laundry out to be washed. The cruise line also touted "country club" casual, no dresses, jackets, or ties, and no formal nights. That is my kind of travel!

I canceled my previously booked 2021 around the world cruise and booked with SeaSpirit on the Luna. This six-hundred-foot ship holds six hundred and seventy passengers and four hundred crew and will sail in 2022. That turned out to be a fortuitous decision, as passengers on all the 2021 world cruises had their trips abruptly canceled and had issues getting home due to Covid19.

CHAPTER 2

Planning First Attempt

NOW that my 2022 world cruise was booked, I was ridiculously excited and had eighteen months to plan and prepare. Now, don't get me wrong. I am a planner and made it my career. Still, I never understood how many details would be involved in preparing for this journey.

When booking, the cruise line presented some "overland excursions." These are several days in length and involve nights in a hotel. This allows for a more in-depth look at a particular place or the time to travel to areas too far removed from a port of call. After choosing overland tours, I researched each of the sixty-four ports I would visit. Being a Libra, I need to weigh all my options, not just see what is offered. I used the library and several websites to find the "must-see" landmarks, cultural venues, and natural history attractions (always my priority). Most of the excursions I wanted were available via the SeaSpirit shore excursion offerings. This is the safest option. Going with a third party is risky; if you do not return to the ship by departure time, the ship leaves without you, and you must catch up to the ship on your own. If you are on the ship's shore excursion, they must wait for you or catch you up to the ship. I wanted to make sure I was never left behind.

I now had to wait a year for my cruise departure. It went agonizingly slow. But during this time, my best friend Harry sold his home in the Midwest to move in with his dad, who needed assistance. Harry would be a perfect traveling companion since we had gone on many cruises together and got along well. He is the only person I know I would ever consider sharing a small cabin with for six months. After a few weeks of soul searching, Harry wholeheartedly accepted my invitation, and we started planning together.

Harry and I have known each other for thirty years. We met on the job. He is as meticulously organized as I am and loves his spreadsheets. He is twelve years my junior and looks like it. People have questioned our relationship every time we go on a cruise together. You can see it on their faces when they look at us. You know they are trying to figure out why we traveled together. Some dare to ask directly, which is an admirable trait. We have made a game of it. We respond with "friends," "lovers," or "business partners," depending on our moods. When people ask if Harry is my son, it pisses me off and makes me feel old. I would have been twelve years old when I delivered him. This has become a bad joke between us; when Harry is in a teasing mood, he calls me "mom."

Harry and I complement each other well in most things. I am more of a worrier, and he is always calm and collected (at least on the outside). I knew if I got on a ledge, Harry would talk me down and make me see a more reasonable approach. His quiet, unassuming nature is soothing when I am concerned about something. Harry looks backward and knows the exact date of all the crucial events in his life; I barely remember the date of my birthday. I look to the future and plan things well in advance, Harry plans for tomorrow, today (literally). Harry is also a couch potato and works a desk job all day. He has a speedy metabolism, whereas I have no metabolism at all. I am always cold; he is always hot. He is remarkably flexible. It seems as if he has double-jointed hips. I have an artificial hip. We like doing lots of the same things. I was totally comfortable going on this cruise with Harry.

CHAPTER 3

The Preparation

HOW do you pack for living six months in such a tiny space? SeaSpirit shipped two fifty-pound suitcases from our homes to the ship and back. Since we were flying to Los Angeles to meet the ship, we decided to take a carry-on for the LA flight and ship everything else. The carry-on would also be used during overland tours.

It all worked out well. We gauged how much shampoo, toothpaste, soap, and other products we would need for six months and weighed all that. Then, we weighed shoes, hats, and jackets. The space and weight remaining were what we allowed for clothes. Thankfully, the SeaSpirit Luna was all about "country club casual," so no formal clothes were needed. Harry and I had to take fewer clothes than we would have liked, but our shipped suitcases weighed forty-eight and fifty pounds. Our carry-ons were very heavy, but those have no weight limit.

We both had Covid19 vaccinations as close to sailing as possible and ensured we had enough medications and a first aid kit. We hoped we had not forgotten anything and thought we were ready to set sail.

CHAPTER 4

The First Departure

A T long last, my four-year quest to take an around the world
cruise had arrived. We flew to Los Angeles, were met by
SeaSpirit staff at the airport, and whisked away to the Four Seasons
Beverly Wilshire Hotel for the night. Somehow, the hotel had put
Harry and me in different rooms. What a happy accident! His room
had a balcony, and mine had two bathrooms. Both were all gleaming
marble. So much opulence for a night's sleep. However, we appreciated
the luxury since we knew we would be in a tiny space every night for
six months.

Reality hit when we awoke and went down to the buffet breakfast
that SeaSpirit provided; Covid19 was still an issue. We understood before
leaving home that there would be virus precautions and interaction rules
and protocols we would need to follow once onboard. We always had
to wear masks except for eating, drinking, or being in our cabin. And
no ship staff would enter our cabin if we were in it. We also understood
that there would be testing before we embarked and disembarked at
some ports of call.

Our first hurdle was pier-side Covid19 testing. I was nervous on
the bus ride to the port. If we were Covid19 positive, we would be left
behind. We checked in, were given a private testing number, and had
a nasal swab taken. We then took a seat. The staff posted completed
test numbers on a screen, and when yours was posted, you could board
the ship. My inner worrying self was in a panic. I knew I drove Harry
crazy as I kept a running dialogue about what I saw happening around
us. He, of course, was his usual stoic self until he finally was over my
babbling and told me nicely to "be quiet; what will be, will be." As we
sat in the waiting room, a staff member pulled a woman aside, quietly

spoke to her, and she disappeared forever. Harry and I looked at each other with disbelief and fear. My panic level went up a notch. What if this happened to us?

Our private number was posted on the screen after what seemed like hours but was more like thirty-five minutes. Thank goodness. Hurdle one removed. We could board. As we walked up the gangway to the red carpet on the deck of the Luna, we heard "Welcome aboard!" spoken by a fifty-something couple in wildly colorful clothes. Paulina, with a purple sequined headband in her glorious red hair, and Charles in a bright jacket and his jet-black round spectacles. They introduced themselves with distinct British accents, informed us they were the host and hostess for our epic journey, and told us we should talk to them if we had any issues. Both are West End theater folks. Paulina is a stage and screen actress, and Charles is an accomplished piano player. The pair had developed a famous raunchy cabaret act renowned in London. As we were talking, a staff member provided a tray of champagne. What a wonderful greeting. As Harry and I clicked our glasses together in our first toast of many, I got butterflies of excitement. It was really happening!

We quickly arrived at our tiny cabin and were utterly surprised and happy; our shipped luggage awaited us. But so was a letter from SeaSpirit. We came to hate the door mail from the cruise line that was not an invitation to dinner or a party. This was not good news. Australia was off the itinerary as it had not opened its borders for tourism yet due to Covid19. We were both disappointed, but Harry more so, as this was on his bucket list, and I had been there previously. But this made everything clear; it was all out of our control.

We decided the best course of action was to unpack and get it over with. Since the cabin was small, one of us needed to stay on a bed while the other unpacked. When everything we could fit in drawers, closets, and cabinets was stowed, the leftover items were stored under the beds in our suitcases. It was cramped, but it was well worth a bit of claustrophobia for an adventure of a lifetime.

CHAPTER 5

Life at Sea

OUR first port of call was Hawaii, so we spent five days at sea exploring the wonders of the Luna. First was happy hour in the One Eighty Lounge and then dinner in the main dining room. Due to Covid19, we both agreed before we boarded that we would not socialize and we would keep our distance from fellow passengers. The last thing we wanted was to contract the virus.

On the first sea day, we started a routine that would stay with us throughout the adventure. We would head upstairs to the buffet for breakfast when we got up in the morning. I got hooked on sticky buns, and Harry loved the omelet station with twelve different add-ins. I then went to find my "spot" on the outside pool deck or up to the Thalassotherapy pool, where it was quiet and secluded to do my puzzles (Wordle, sudoku, and coloring) and to people-watch. Harry joined some days, and others, he would take a yoga class.

Most mornings, Luna offered "enrichment" activities. There was usually a talk about some area pertinent to where we were in the world. Sometimes, it was cultural, sometimes geographical, and sometimes about the natural history of a location. Some speakers were enlightening and engaging, and others were not. I attended some that appealed to me, and I enjoyed them. Harry skipped most. They also have an art room with a resident artist onboard with us. Art classes included portrait painting, watercolors, beading, and necklace making. None of the choices appealed to either of us. I am more of a crafter than an artist, and Harry is neither.

One of my favorite spots on the Luna was the Thalassotherapy pool, outside at the front of the ship in the spa. This type of pool uses heated seawater, rich in minerals such as magnesium, potassium, and calcium, to promote health and well-being. Soaking in this mineral-rich, heated, bubbling seawater allows the skin to absorb essential elements, enhancing circulation and alleviating muscle and joint pain. This area was "reserved" for guests in suites, which was not me. However, this tiny area was empty most days, so no one ever hassled me about enjoying the space. And I loved it. It was one of my happy places.

After the spa, I would shower, dress for my afternoon activities, and then head to lunch. After lunch, Harry would go to the gym or walk on the outdoor track. He set quite an ambitious goal during the voyage to walk a million and a half miles. My goal was markedly different. I am an avid Texas Hold'em tournament-style poker player who has honed my skills for years. Before boarding, I knew the ship had a small casino, so I did not expect live poker, let alone Texas Hold'em tournaments. This was a wonderful surprise. I was excited to see how many players we would have on the first day. Turns out we had plenty. James, Jose, and Patty became friends as we played countless games. So, anyone looking for me on a sea day at 2 pm could find me in the casino. My goal was to come home with poker money in my pocket.

After poker, I had a bit of a lie-down for reading or napping, and then I would change for dinner and head up to the One Eighty Lounge for drinks and people-watching. They had live music in the lounge every night, and there were quite a few wonderful dance couples who I enjoyed watching. The band was excellent, and the band leader had a penchant for jazz, my favorite.

After the drinks, we would go to dinner. We had five choices of where and how we wanted to eat. The evening buffet, the main dining room, Bistro Italiano or Prime Grille. The Grille and Bistro, specialty restaurants, were reservations only. We had limited bookings, which we took full advantage of, but most nights, we ate in the main dining room. Harry and I both preferred to be served as opposed to the buffet. The last dining option is 24/7 room service. Occasionally, one of us would choose this option, and a few times, we both had dinner in the cabin and watched a movie together.

After dinner there is always a "show" in the Stage Left Theater. Four singers and two dancers were part of the entertainment staff. Still, most of the shows were short-term contracts with many different performers. These performers would board and do two shows over three days with the middle day off. They booked jugglers, comics, magicians, singers, instrumentalists, dancers, cultural performances, you name it. I am jaded when it comes to entertainment and have no patience for what I have termed "amateur hour." Harry chose to attend often, me not so much. When I decided to go, I always sat in the back row near the door so I could sneak out when I had my fill, which occurred often. Harry has a lot more patience than I do.

CHAPTER 6

The North Pacific Gyre

T HE North Pacific Ocean Gyre is a group of ocean currents that circulate clockwise around the entire Pacific basin. It is critical for the marine ecosystem and the regulation of ocean temperature. Due to its presence, the Northern Pacific Ocean tends to have rough seas. One of the Enrichment Speakers spent an hour educating all of us on this phenomenon; fifteen minutes would have sufficed.

Our time crossing the Pacific Ocean was not pleasant for me. I am prone to seasickness. I want to lie down in one place and not move. I have no sea legs. On the other hand, Harry wishes for a bad storm and high seas. I had brought medication with me, but the Meclizine that the ship provided worked the best if I took half a tablet before bed and then had a Coke in the morning to help with the residual drowsiness.

On the third sea day, we received an invitation to a Captain's Cocktail Party. We discovered that a cocktail party was in store at the beginning of every segment. The world cruise had about three hundred passengers circumnavigating the globe and other passengers that would join for a portion called a segment. Harry coined the term "oranges" when referring to passengers on one or more segments. Honestly, we were being catty with this term. Oranges have segments, and we wanted a word we could freely use in public without listeners knowing what we were talking about.

As was our custom, I showered, changed for dinner, and joined the cocktail party, and then Harry did the same. This gave us both some privacy in our tiny cabin. Before Harry joined me, I had found a private table for two. We continued to isolate ourselves due to Covid19. I ordered a drink, and as this was the "Captain's" party, he provided an open bar. While waiting for my drink, Paulina stopped by to check on me, asking if I was alright. I suspect she was concerned because I was by myself. After we chatted for a bit, Paulina flitted off to another table, and then another. I am sure she stopped at every table during the party. She obviously took her hostess duties seriously.

During our time in the Northern Pacific, we crossed the equator. There is a ritual for all Polliwogs (first-time equator crossers by sea), including a ceremony asking permission from King Neptune and his court. Participants must kiss a three-foot dead mackerel, kneel to King Neptune, and be anointed with ice water while saying "Holy Mackerel." After the ceremony, Polliwogs officially became "Shellbacks" and received a certificate to prove it. Hopefully, King Neptune will provide calmer seas moving forward.

CHAPTER 7

Hawaii and the South Pacific – Whales and Shades of Turquoise

Oahu, Hawaii

HARRY and I decided to go to Pearl Harbor on our day in Oahu. I had been there before, and I remembered how moving it was. The grounds of the USS Arizona Memorial are a park with heart-felt stories placed along a picturesque walkway lined with flowering bushes. Walking this pathway reminds us about the cost of freedom. Over eleven hundred lives were lost here. The memorial is a floating bridge over the battleship; the only way to get there is by boat. The bridge has twenty-one openings to represent a twenty-one-gun salute for our fallen soldiers. It was just as moving to me as the first time I visited.

Kahului, Maui

We rented a car in Kahului. When we got to the rental agency, they told us to take whichever car we wanted. Harry is always the designated driver since I look at the scenery too much and am not good at doing two things at once. He chose a Mustang convertible.

With the top down, we went to Lahaina, Maui, halfway around the small island. The ride was breathtaking, as the road hugged the coast with the mountains on one side and the ocean on the other. We saw whales spouting and breaching all the way to Lahaina.

We arrived early in Lahaina for our afternoon whale watch, so we wandered around Front Street, which dates to the 1820s. It is lined with stores and restaurants. Off Front Street is Banyan Court Park, the main attraction of which is a huge banyan tree planted by William Owen Smith in April 1873. The tree is huge and fills the whole park. We sat under that tree for quite a while. When I heard about the 2023 fire that destroyed Lahaina, I thought about that tree. As the fire's first anniversary has passed, I am happy to say that the first restored house is complete, and the tree still survives.

When it was time for our whale watch, we headed to the dock to check in. Since we were early, we could pick our seats on the zodiac. With Harry's quick thinking and feet, we got the only two seats facing toward the boat's bow. The other seats faced off to one side or the other. After a quick safety talk, we were going for a two-hour ride to search for humpback whales.

Throughout the first hour, we saw a few whales come to the surface and a few tails out of the water. I was furiously taking pictures at every glimpse of every whale. My camera was new for the trip and had a 100x zoom lens, so I was the designated picture taker. About ninety minutes in, my arms and hands were tired from taking pictures, and Harry offered to take over for me. Another fortuitous event. I had been taking selfies all that time. My photographs were not of whales but of me. During the last thirty minutes, we were lucky enough to see one whale breach three times about ten feet away from our little boat. Harry got the shots. Breathtaking. It was an incredible experience to be so close to these creatures. I also learned an important lesson about using my camera. I also had to delete hundreds of pictures of me.

Kona, Hawaii

Our last day in Hawaii was in Kona, on the big island. My one and only college roommate lives there, and we do not get to see each other often. We spent the day catching up during the two-hour drive back and forth between Volcano National Park and her home. Unfortunately, the volcano was covered in fog, so we could not see much. But it was an enjoyable day until we returned to our cabin and received the dreaded cabin mail.

We had an official SeaSpirit letter stating that due to Covid19, the countries west of us were not yet open to visitors. The Luna had to turn around after French Polynesia and return to Los Angeles. My heart sank! All the planning and dreaming was for naught. SeaSpirit did give us a choice after arriving in LA. We could get off the ship and fly home or continue with the Luna, going east to the Mexican Riviera, the Caribbean, up the coast of South America, and then north to Europe. We had previously traveled to that side of the world, so we both quickly agreed to disembark in Los Angeles.

It was time to pivot as quickly as possible since there were now three hundred-plus passengers searching for alternative cruises. The SeaSpirit 2023 world cruise was sold out. That itinerary was going east around the globe and included South America, so I did not even put us on the waitlist. The 2024 cruise was going west to the Middle East instead of Africa, so that would have to do. During our short time aboard Luna, I learned all about cabin placement. Due to my seasickness issues, I now knew I needed a midship cabin. Not one at the bow of the ship where each time the vessel climbed a wavefront, I felt it. So, our 2024 cabin was in the middle of the middle. I hoped it would help with my queasiness. Harry had absolutely no preference.

French Polynesia

Before we headed home, we visited French Polynesia, including Tahiti, Bora Bora, Rangiora, Raiatea, and Moorea in the South Pacific. I had visited before, but this was Harry's first time. I consider this paradise on Earth. Many small, lush, tropical islands close together, surrounded by a gazillion colors of turquoise seas. Describing the beauty of the water is impossible. I thought maybe my obsession with being on the water there was unique to me, but Harry caught the same bug. Catamarans were the best way to surround ourselves with this beauty. I don't recall how many sailings we did, but they included swimming with black-tipped sharks, feeding sting rays, snorkeling, and sunset cruises, to name a few. It was all mesmerizing.

Then, we went back to reality in more ways than one. Thirty-four days after we left Los Angeles for the adventure of a lifetime, we ended up right where we started. Now, I needed to restart my life at home and wait another two years to follow my dream. I started planning.

CHAPTER 8

The Second Departure and Life Onboard

A GAIN, Harry and I planned and packed our bags and set off for Los Angeles in the middle of January 2024. I felt like I had been in limbo for two years, wasting away the days until it was time. The significant change between 2024 and 2022 was that Covid19 was no longer a deadly issue; no pre-board testing or always wearing masks when we were not in our cabin. We landed in LA, took the SeaSpirit transfer to the Beverly Wilshire Four Season Hotel, and checked in. We were a bit disappointed when they gave us one room and not two, but it was a spacious, opulent room, so we were not that disappointed. In 2022, we tried to get reservations for dinner at Musso & Frank Grill and failed, but we had lots of time to prepare, so we did succeed in 2024.

Harry heard about this restaurant when he was visiting a friend who took him to the Emmy Awards, and he had it on his bucket list to dine there. I had seen it in a Bosch episode, and I was immediately in. The Grill is the oldest restaurant in town, established in 1919 during the heyday of Hollywood. I was ready to see the rich and famous enjoying the fettuccine alfredo, the restaurant's signature dish. This pasta dish was made using Douglas Fairbanks Jr. and Mary Pickford's recipe from Italy. The food was delicious and the atmosphere fantastic, but we recognized no one.

In the morning, we were again treated to a buffet breakfast, a bus ride to the pier, and a not-so-smooth check-in process. Then, we were back on the red carpet as we boarded the Luna. And as in 2022, I spotted flaming red hair with a purple sequined headband and heard "welcome aboard" in a familiar British accent. This time, however, there were hugs from Paulina and Charles, who were back as the host and hostess of the 2024 world cruise. That moment made it real for me. We were back on track for the adventure of a lifetime. We all toasted with champagne, and the hair on my arms stood up.

We then proceeded to our middle cabin and were pleasantly surprised to find that our luggage had arrived. We had learned a few things from 2022 and had come prepared with hanging storage shelves, shoe bags, and magnets to hang them with. These turned out to be very useful. We unpacked and set up the room.

Poker

Again, I looked forward to the afternoon poker tournament every sea day. The first would set the players and determine if we would have sufficient players to make it a game. On the first day, we had seven players. James, from Las Vegas; Patty, from Miami; and Jose, from Castagna, Columbia, all of whom I had met and played with in 2022. Patty was having concentration issues and only played with us twice. Still, it was wonderful to spend time with her at the Thalassotherapy pool most mornings. Also joining us was Dexter from Las Vegas, Sukie from Savannah, and Olaf and Inga, a Swedish couple who were good players and hilarious to play with. Every time Inga had to add money to the pot to start the blinds, she would say in her heavy Scandinavian accent, "It hurts," which got us all giggling and made it not hurt so much when it came to our own turns to pay for the blinds.

Trivia

Every afternoon, there was Team Trivia with the Cruise Director, Judy. Harry and I did not participate in 2022 because of Covid19 precautions, but we had no issue in 2024. I knew it was something I wanted to do. Harry was not sure but eventually came around. It took me several attempts to get on the right team. Harry waited to join until he had zeroed in on the one team that met his high standards.

Unsurprisingly, we ended up on the same team, but I had to offer him a bribe to be allowed to join his team.

The rules were simple: a maximum of eight people were on each team, and no cell phones or laptops could be used. Judy was "always right," even if her "correct" answer was questionable. They gave prizes daily to the top three teams, and we won "S" points, which could be spent on SeaSpirit logo merchandise at the end of every segment. Toward the end of the cruise, when the passengers walked down the gangway at ports of call, many passengers wore logo hats, shirts, socks, and jackets. It appeared like we all played for the same team, and I guess we did. SeaSpirit was no dummy when it came to advertising. It was unexpectedly helpful; you could quickly identify fellow passengers if you got lost and just follow the line of SeaSpirit jackets to the bus.

Judy was good at controlling the sometimes rowdy crowd with up to ten teams of eight. She and the entertainment staff had to come up with over twenty-five hundred questions and answers over the six months, and they did not make them easy. Our team was full of highly competitive players, including myself. Judy loved to stump the room. If there was a lot of buzz after a question, Judy would ask each team for their answer. When none of the teams got a question correct, she said in her midwestern accent, "you learn something new every day." Even today, when I learn something new, which I love to do, I hear her voice in my head!

Our team, named the Above Boards, had eight players. Steve and his husband Gayle are from Denver. Steve was the best among us; his memory is incredible. As an actor and reader, he knows everything about the entertainment arena. Gayle was our finance and business guru and our scribe. He brought calmness to our madness and was the final arbitrator if we could not agree on the answer. Monte, a friend of Gayle's from Chicago and an ex-monk turned hospital administrator could answer any religious or British history-related question. Gladys, an office manager, and her husband Lincoln, a physician who knew anatomy, physiology, and all things medical. Theresa, an educator with a broad range of knowledge, had her two children aboard and was "home" schooling them and finishing her PH.D. Harry knows all about today's pop culture and voluntarily took to memorizing the collective nouns, such as a parliament of owls. I brought my medical background and love of the natural world to the team. We collected a few "S" points and satisfied my competitiveness most days.

Gang of Seven

Now that Harry and I were socializing with other passengers, we quickly found a group of seven that we bonded with. We would meet in the One Eighty Lounge most nights before dinner for drinks. We would share our day, discuss where we would eat dinner, not usually all together, but in an ever-changing configuration. We would then discuss our plans for the next day. This way, we could get our bus tickets together if we were going on the same excursion, if we so chose. Bonding with this group was an unexpected bonus. I never expected to make lifelong friends on this journey. Steve, Gayle, Monte, Catherine, Bob, Harry, and I made up the "gang." Catherine and Bob are retired businesspeople from Palm Springs, California. They have and continue to travel extensively and know how to travel well. As the adventure went on, I used to joke that I needed a social secretary to keep track of the excursions off the ship, drinks, and/or dinner invitations, as well as cocktail parties.

CHAPTER 9

Hawaii – Refuge and Waves

A S we left Los Angeles for the first segment of the second attempt on the world cruise, I had high expectations for our first ports of call in Hawaii and French Polynesia. Harry and I had plans to spend a day with my college roommate, spend time on the North Shore of Oahu, return to Volcano National Park, and enjoy sailing around the Marquises Islands. We were not disappointed.

Kona, Hawaii

I had been under the weather for a few days with weird congestion affecting my throat. This would be a recurring issue for me, but the first time I got it, I was unsure if it was a cold or an allergy. I tried hard to ignore it as we headed out to see my college roommate, who had lived on the big island for several decades. She picked Harry and me up at the tender dock. She drove us to the City of Refuge, Pu'uhonua o Honaunau National Historical Park. The Hawaiian political system was restricted in ancient times, and penalties were severe. Still, if you could make it to a refuge, it would provide a safe haven as granted by the priests. The sanctuary sits on an outcrop surrounded by a tranquil, protected bay. The black sand and lava beach were in sharp contrast to the cerulean blue of the sea and the sky, with not a cloud in sight. I felt at peace in this stunning place.

Hilo, Hawaii

Harry and I rented a car in Hilo and made our second visit to Volcano National Park. Thankfully, there was no fog, and we could see the crater of Kilauea, one of the most active volcanoes on Earth. It last erupted before our visit in 2022 and has since erupted in 2025. The crater was massive, with many vents spewing steam. We were overwhelmed by the smell of rotting eggs from the sulfur being expelled into the air. It was something to behold.

Harry then descended a steep, slippery hill with questionable handrails to a series of lava tubes. I knew this was not something I was not willing to venture into, but I was sure Harry would love it. He described it as a long circular tunnel made of jet-black rippled lava. He said he could stand upright in most places, but there were a few places where he had to bend so as not to hit his head. The floor was all rippled and challenging to navigate. It was dark with a pinprick of light off in the distance, which, as he approached, grew more prominent. Any light that did come through made the lava glow orange and red. He said it appeared as if the tube was on fire, and it was eerie and beautiful simultaneously. As I predicted, Harry loved it. I am sure he was hoping for some red-hot lava sightings during our time in the park and maybe an earthquake rumble or two, but it was not to be. I, for one, was thankful.

On our way back to meet Luna, we passed the Dole Pineapple Plantation. It is no longer a working farm but a tourist destination. It is renowned for its Pineapple Whip. The best way to describe this creamy treat is soft ice cream flavored intensely with pineapple. You can order this pure or mix it with cookies and candy favorites. Harry and I elected the purist variety. It was well worth the visit.

North Shore of Oahu, Hawaii

The North Shore is renowned for its world-class surfing beaches, attracting surfers from around the globe. We rented a car and drove about an hour to the island's north end. We were disappointed in 2022 since we took a Luna shore excursion; the surf was not very high, and the bus could not stop. This time, it did not disappoint; it was high surf with lots of surfers. We stopped many times and watched the waves and surfers. We went to the famous Banzai Pipeline, one of the world's most famous and challenging surf breaks. It is known for its powerful, fast-breaking waves forming pipes as they crash onto the reef. We saw surfers in the pipe, and they made it out safely without being wiped out.

CHAPTER 10

The South Pacific – Chargers, Warm Waters, Bats and Covid19

AFTER we departed Hawaii, we had five sea days before we reached Tahiti. Life onboard the Luna resumed. During our time in Hawaii, my congestion did not get better. It was now affecting my sleep as I would wake up in the middle of the night choking, which also woke Harry. After coaxing from Harry, I went down to the sickbay to talk to the doctor. It was quite a busy place. The first thing they did was test me for Covid19. I was nervous; I had never had the virus, so I did not know what it felt like. After ten minutes of waiting impatiently, they said I was Covid19 free. The doctor then prescribed an over-the-counter cold medication that I had already been taking, cough medicine, and a course of steroids, which I knew would do the trick, and it did.

During dinner with the gang, I described my visit to the doctor and my mysterious illness and jokingly named my ailment "kennel cough". Everything on a small ship spreads like wildfire, whether it is a virus, rumors, or corroborated facts. By lunch the next day, from a group of four passengers sitting behind me, with whom I had no contact, I heard someone mention they thought they had "kennel cough." I was shocked to hear the term but should not have been.

The day before we reached Tahiti, I went to recharge my electric toothbrush and could not locate the charger. Harry and I searched everywhere to no avail. I used it the night before our flight and must have returned it to the drawer where it usually belongs instead of packing it. I need routines, but occasionally they become detrimental. I had a manual toothbrush with me which would need to work temporarily until I found a way to purchase a charger, my first preference, or buy a new electric toothbrush.

I had an idea that I could buy a charger on Amazon and send it to the ship in one of the major cities we were going to visit. I spoke to the purser, who gave me the name and email address of the Port Agent in Sydney, Australia. He suggested I reach out for direction, which I did. He gave me the process to follow, and I ordered a replacement charger on Amazon and then kept my fingers crossed.

Tahiti

There is nothing like being on the crystal-clear aquamarine waters of the South Pacific. These islands are close together and are coral atolls, making the water around them shallow. Hence, the white sand ocean bed is easily visible. Harry and I sailed on the sixty-five-foot catamaran for a snorkeling trip down the west coast of Tahiti. This catamaran has netting out over the water on the bow, Harry's happy place. After an hour of cruising, we dropped anchor and jumped into the eighty-five-degree water for playtime with sting rays and black-tipped sharks. The boat captain was hand-feeding these youngsters, and we were amazed observers. These animals surrounded us, which was scary but quite exhilarating as well. We loved it!

Bora Bora

Another spectacular day on the seafoam water in a catamaran. We were on a smaller "cat," which could skirt the coastline, getting into secluded coves and remarkably close to the overwater bungalows that are iconic in pictures of Bora Bora. From here, we could enjoy an excellent view of Mount Otemanu, one of two extinct volcanoes rising from the center of the lush green island. Soon, we were again in the water, snorkeling over a reef teeming with coral and fish.

In the afternoon, we took a cab to the most famous restaurant in French Polynesia, Bloody Mary's. They are renowned for fresh seafood, a sand-covered floor, uncomfortable tree stump seats, and a tropical take on the Bloody Mary cocktail. This is also where you might run into a celebrity of two. Johnny Depp, Brad Pitt, and Jimmy Buffett have all been spotted here. I could not understand why the restaurant was such a draw. The seats are terribly uncomfortable. It seemed the owners were trying to get their patrons to eat quickly and leave. The fresh Mahi was delicious, though. On the way out was a tiny gift shop, and both Harry and I got tee shirts. I picked up two ball caps for friends from home. Unfortunately, we recognized no celebrities.

In all my visits to these islands, I am always in awe of nature's beauty of the land and seascapes. How much time can you spend sailing on a catamaran in the aqua waters in the South Pacific, paradise itself? If you are like Harry and I, there is never enough time. This is my paradise on Earth.

As we departed these islands, I heard from my college roommate that she was extremely sick with long Covid19. It would take her four months to recover. I had dodged a huge bullet. Harry and I could have been exposed when we visited, or we could have been responsible for getting her sick. Thank goodness, neither was the case.

Suva, Fiji, Melanesia

Our first stop was to Thurston Gardens. When we arrived at the gardens, I thought we were in amongst a flock of noisy parrots, but it turned out to be a big roosting colony of flying foxes, the largest of the fruit bats. They can be two feet tall and have a wingspan of five feet. They rest in trees during the day, hanging upside down. They were amazing to see up close with their curious, watchful, amber eyes in black, pointed faces.

We then drove to the Colo-I-Suva Forest Park. As soon as we arrived at the rainforest, it started to rain, but luckily, by the time our guide told us the list of rules, the rain had stopped. However, the path was muddy and slippery due to the heavy rains over the past few days. The hot and humid air made the dense foliage sparkle and glisten. The birds were loud and raucous. As we approached one of the small pools with a picturesque waterfall, Harry walked to the edge to rinse his hands and proceeded to slip in the mud and land on his back. He was lucky to get only his shoes and socks wet. As I lent him a hand, he quietly swore under his breath, which is unlike him. The hike back to the bus was unpleasant for him because of his soaked footwear, which he trashed when we returned to the ship. Before leaving the park, we were handed a bottle of Fiji water. Very fitting.

We now had five sea days before we reached New Zealand. Harry woke up the first morning coughing and sneezing. He thought it was his yearly head cold, but I suggested he visit the sick bay. When he returned to our cabin, he looked crestfallen. He had tested positive for Covid19. This was his third case since 2021. He instructed me to leave the cabin immediately. He told me to "go wait someplace for an hour" while he packed and was moved to a balcony cabin, where they locked him in for his three days of quarantine. Really! At least I would have a cabin to myself during that time. He was given upgraded wi-fi for free so he could stream videos. He said he did not feel too ill, and that never changed during his seclusion, thank goodness. If this had to happen, the timing could not have been better as he was only missing sea days. He spent his time in isolation catching up on a month's worth of The Young and The Restless, which he also recorded at home. The doctor required that I get tested and monitored for Covid19 every morning. Thankfully, I never got sick.

CHAPTER 11

International Dateline

WE knew we would cross this mind-boggling milestone, and so we did. Sometime in the middle of the night, we lost twenty-four hours of our lives, which we would gain back hour by hour on a more than weekly basis by setting our clocks back. I have never been good with time changes. My body's circadian rhythm needs weeks to sort itself out, whether from jet lag or daylight savings time. It has never been easy for me. Thank goodness for Harry; he was the designated time management guru and set our cabin clock every few days to the appropriate time.

I am not alone in having time issues. Many passengers were cranky and lagging, even though we had gotten an hour of extra sleep in the morning after these changes. Me included. Those days, caffeinated Coca-Cola was my morning beverage of choice.

CHAPTER 12

New Zealand – Worms, Mud, Gannets, and a Blizzard

I WAS in New Zealand for my fortieth birthday when I visited Australia. The focus of my visit all those years ago was to see the incredible wildlife of Australia. The journey I chose included New Zealand, but I expected it to be the same as Australia, which was a total fallacy. When I returned home after my first visit, I knew I wanted to find my way back.

Kawiti, North Island

One of the natural wonders of New Zealand is the glow worm caves. I have known about them for years, and they have always been on my bucket list. There are several caves in New Zealand where the worms are easily accessible. Still, all the sites are strictly controlled for the safety of the worms and the humans wandering around in dark caves. We went to Kawiti. These caves have been owned by the same Māori family for hundreds of years. They have made getting into the caves and seeing the worms easy. They built stairways and platforms around the cave's sides to cause the worms the least disturbance.

Glow worms are not actually worms but the bio-luminescent larvae of flies. They produce light through a chemical reaction in their bodies, which they use to attract food (mosquitoes, flies, and other small insects). They need to eat one bug every three weeks; I would love that. Once fed, they no longer glow since they have no need to attract bugs, thus saving energy. The cave was impressive, with many calcium carbonate stalagmites and stalactites. As we got deeper into the cave, our guide asked us to stop moving, turn off our lanterns, and look up. It seemed as if we were viewing green constellations in a pitch-black sky. Tiny pinpoints of green light surrounded us. The sight was well worth the wait.

Rotorua, North Island

Rotorua is noted for its geothermal activity due to the volcanic caldera at its center. We chose to go to Hell's Gate Mud Bath Retreat, which has been run by the Māori for generations. We wandered the property on a trail surrounded by pools of bubbling mud, fumaroles spewing sulfur fumes, and steam vents. They were preparing our lunch using steam from the caldera during our stroll. We were then ready for the mud. We wore bathing suits and headed for the first mud pool fit for humans. After we "mudded" each other, we sat in the sun to dry. Then, we went off to the shower to rinse all the mud off and then into a hot water pool, my favorite. We came out glistening since the heated, nutrient-rich mud has a silky-smooth texture that naturally exfoliates, detoxifies, and polishes your skin. That was all good, but my skin smelt like sulfur until I had taken a third shower for the day.

Napier, North Island

Hawke's Bay Cape Kidnapper is home to the largest mainland colony of Australasian gannets. As we approached the colony, the noise and smell gradually intensified. Once we could see the birds, the noise level was deafening, with parents squawking in greeting and chicks clamoring to be fed. The smell of ammonia was overpowering.

Usually, these large sea birds' nest in colonies on cliffs and rocky outcrops along the coast because they need a significant takeoff and landing strip due to their size. After they take off, they also need air under their wings to keep them aloft. They were comical to watch; they are gangly and wobbly and never seem to land quite where they intended to. They are known for their incredible diving and fishing abilities, plunging into the ocean from great heights to catch fish. They are also famous for the ritualized recognition dance performed by mating partners who pair for life. After about four months, the chicks are heavier than their parents and ready to fledge. They wait for a stiff wind, take to the air, and immediately fly the fifteen hundred miles (non-stop) to their wintering grounds. That is why they are heavier than their parents. We stayed with the colony for quite a while and were entertained by their antics and natural behaviors. We were also awed by the setting on this rugged cliff overlooking the sea, which was not a bad place to call home.

Christchurch, South Island

The International Antarctic Centre is a showcase of the natural wonder that is at the bottom of the world. The center features a range of interactive exhibits that allow visitors to experience what life is like in Antarctica. Of note is the indoor polar room that simulates the extreme conditions of weather on the continent. We suited up in heavy coats that were provided and entered a white square room with icy patches on the floor. I was holding on to Harry so as not to fall. The room temperature was a constant seventeen degrees Fahrenheit. Still, the thirty-plus mph howling winds made it feel like one degree below zero. We were in a raging blizzard, and I was happy to leave. Harry did survive the full twenty minutes; I was impressed.

The Centre sits next to the United States Antarctic Program headquarters, which manages the three Antarctic research stations. It is the main gateway to ferry people and supplies to these stations. We were lucky enough to be there as a plane was prepared for a resupply mission.

New Zealand did not disappoint! The place's natural history is astounding, and the people love Americans because they believe we saved their country during WWII. They would literally open their homes to us if we needed shelter. Even though it was on my bucket list to visit again, I could not cross it off just yet, as I would love to go back again and spend some extended time in one or two of their impressive cities.

CHAPTER 13

Australia – Awe, Shark, and Shoes

I WAS looking forward to returning to Australia to spend more time exploring its diverse and odd animal life. It was also a must-see on Harry's bucket list. Neither one of us was disappointed.

Sydney, New South Wales

On the morning of our arrival, we sailed through Sydney Harbor and got spectacular views of the Sydney Opera House, the Sydney Eye, and Luna Park Sydney, the amusement park on the shore. We also went under the famous Sydney Harbor Bridge.

The highlight for me in Sydney was not seeing the remarkable Opera House, Harbor Bridge, or Bondi Beach; I had seen them on my previous trip. Harry did visit all of them. Sydney is one of my favorite cities for its friendliness, relaxed atmosphere, and high energy. I had always wanted to see a performance in the Sydney Opera House. Several of our cruise mates had gotten opera tickets, but as opera is not my favorite and dance was not an option, I got a ticket to see RBG, a one-woman show about Supreme Court Justice Ruth Bader Ginsberg. Since Harry was not at all interested, I was a tad nervous about getting there and back solo, but I should not have been concerned. I took an Uber there and a cab back, and besides the bit of drama finding the cab stand, it was not too traumatic. And the play was well worth the angst. I would not think Australians would be interested in a play about an American public figure, but it was wonderfully received and got four standing ovations!

On our second day in Sydney, we visited a United Nations Educational, Scientific and Cultural Organization (UNESCO) World Heritage site, the Blue Mountains. We boarded a cable car to go down seventeen hundred and eighty-eight feet to Jamieson Valley's rainforest, where we strolled around on our own, intentionally breaking away from the noisy group to seek the quiet for better wildlife sightings. This forest is otherworldly, more like Jurassic Park, with giant ferns damp with mist and twelve-foot-tall palm trees. We were lucky to spot the Superb Lyrebird and a Lewin's Honeyeater amongst the trees.

On the way back up the mountain we took the world's steepest perpendicular railway. It inclines fifty-two degrees with backward-facing seats tilted at a peculiar angle, I felt like I was stuck backwards in a dentist's chair between sitting up and lying down. From there, we boarded a Skyway gondola, which took us eight hundred and eighty-five feet high over the valley with the Blue Mountains in the distance. The panoramic views were awe-inspiring and showed off the majestic Three Sisters rock formations in all their glory. They are three times bigger than the Grand Canyon.

When we returned to the ship, the concierge called to advise me that a package had arrived for me. My toothbrush charger had made it aboard. I have to say, I was happily surprised.

Cairns, Queensland

The Great Barrier Reef is immense, covering an area of approximately one hundred and thirty thousand square miles, the size of Arizona and

Utah combined. It stretches over fourteen hundred and thirty miles and is composed of over twenty-nine hundred individual reefs and nine hundred islands. The reef is known for its incredible biodiversity. It is home to a wide variety of marine life, including over fifteen hundred species of fish, four hundred species of coral, and numerous species of sharks, rays, and marine mammals. For good reason, the Great Barrier Reef is a UNESCO World Heritage site. It is so large it can be seen from space.

I had snorkeled the reef thirty years ago, and I remember jumping off a small boat into crystal-clear waters and seeing lots of fish and coral. What struck me this time was how the tourist industry had gotten very sophisticated to attract and service large numbers of visitors every day. From the Luna, we walked over to a large catamaran that took us to a private pontoon floating atop the outer reef. While docked at the pontoon, the catamaran served as our storage area and bathroom, and we could quickly go between them during our stay on the reef. The pontoon had many options for viewing the world's richest marine habitat. There was diving, snorkeling, glass bottom boat viewing, a submersible trip, and several underwater viewing platforms on the pontoon.

Harry and I booked a "shelf" dive, and as we waited for that group to depart, we took advantage of all the other options on the pontoon and had the provided lunch. When the dive master was ready for us, we donned wetsuits and gear and headed to the edge of the pontoon platform, where we jumped into the calm, warm water. We swam over a reef teeming with fish and coral in vibrant hues of greens, pinks, and purples. Then, the reef abruptly ended and dropped off into the abyss; we had made it to the "shelf." As we swam down the vertical reef, we saw a different array of corals and the small fish sheltered among them.

As Harry and I were heading deeper, we turned a blind corner and faced a scary and odd-looking six-foot hammerhead shark. I get calm when I get myself in a situation of absolute panic. The flood of adrenaline affects me differently than most, and it has always turned out to be a good thing. Hammerheads are not usually aggressive toward humans unless provoked or threatened, but I did not know that then.

It seemed like the shark was studying me with its strangely spaced eyes. It was unnerving, to say the least. Harry looked at me with fear, but I gave him the thumbs-up sign and signaled we should slowly backpedal and give the shark all the space he needed. We made it out of the water with all our limbs attached and a good story.

Newcastle, New South Wales

As this incredible adventure continued, I got physically fitter, some days walking more than five miles. Thus, I found myself in dire need of a good pair of walking shoes. For years, I have worn the same brand of shoes, and right before we set sail, they were no longer comfortable, and I struggled to replace them. I thought I had found a brand that would work, but that was not the case. I wore an old, broken-down pair every day when we were off the ship and did not see how they would last until we made it to New York.

The day was cool and drizzling, one of the few days we were impacted by bad weather. I researched and found a shoe store in town that was open on Sunday. I boarded the Luna shuttle into town, walked the few blocks to the store, and had my fingers crossed the entire time. I successfully bought a pair of shoes.

When I boarded the ship, Paulina greeted me with a hug and said, "Welcome home." It took me a moment for that statement to register, but then it struck just the right chord. The Luna did feel like a home to me. I shared that sentiment with Harry when he made it back from his excursion, and he agreed. It became natural for us to call the Luna home.

When I got to my cabin, I immediately put on my new shoes. Not one hour later, I tripped and fell out of the elevator, almost falling headfirst down the stairs. Luckily, several passengers on the elevator assisted, and I did not get hurt. I immediately relegated the shoes to the laundry bag under my bed. What was I going to do with all these useless shoes?

CHAPTER 14

More Dreaded Mail

AFTER dinner, we had unwanted mail waiting for us in the cabin. It was not unexpected news. We had been watching the events occurring in the Middle East before we departed Los Angeles. Many other cruise lines had already canceled their voyages to that part of the world. We had been holding our breaths for quite some time to see what SeaSpirit would do. Passengers constantly discussed possible options for an itinerary change. I did not want to traverse the Red Sea because it was unsafe, and I would love to return to Africa, so that was my choice. Harry had not been to Africa or the Middle East, so he had no preference but was wary of the events happening in the Red Sea.

The letter spelled out the new itinerary, which excluded the entire Middle Eastern and Mediterranean legs. Instead, it went around Africa and crossed the Atlantic to the U.S. This was a logistical nightmare for the cruise line. Dock space, ship provisioning, and a million other needs are planned and booked months in advance. SeaSpirit did a good job of providing us with an alternative itinerary without canceling a third of our cruise. This new itinerary had more sea days and less ports of call.

Suzette, the ship's manager, hosted a meeting with the captain, concierges, and the host and hostess, with all the affected passengers for a question-and-answer session. The passengers were quite vocal in the meeting and made it clear that some were unhappy with the changes and some were downright angry. Due to malaria concerns, some did not want to go to Africa, specifically West Africa. Others wanted SeaSprirt to find a way to fit in more ports and fewer sea days. Others chose this cruise for the Middle Eastern segment and wanted to go no matter the risks. SeaSpirit did provide some financial credit for a future voyage because of the reduced number of ports of call, but they made it clear that refunds would not be provided if you chose to get off the ship early. Luna would give prophylactic malaria medications or letters of exclusion to everyone.

My biggest concern was how we would all choose overland tours and shore excursions fairly and equitably. Usually, these are offered on a first-come, first-served basis, but with three new segments and many ports, the people in the front would have the first choice of everything, and if you were last, you would get nothing. After the meeting, the staff agreed to take that concern under advisement. SeaSpirit settled on offering a lottery system for each segment, which saved us from standing in line for hours, and that seemed fair to me.

Harry is the lucky one, and I had him draw the number for the first segment, overland tours and East Africa, which were my biggest concerns. He picked a low number, and we got all our choices for the first segment. Harry made me choose for the second segment, South and West Africa, but I was not lucky. We were south of the middle but got most of our first choices. Harry picked for the last segment, and we were at the end of the pack. We ended up with no shore excursions booked with SeaSpirit. That meant we needed to get busy with more research to find alternatives.

After the meeting, a few passengers signed a petition insisting that they get a refund if they decided to shorten their cruise. The petition was presented to Suzette, who agreed to send it to corporate but doubted any positive results. Suzette also gave the signed petition to Paulina, and she individually met with the signers to find out the details of their concerns. This extra effort did lead to some medical concerns being rectified. She also identified a cancellation clause in the European passenger contract, allowing them refunds if they chose to leave the ship early. Unfortunately, the disgruntled Americans had no recourse; they would either stay aboard or lose money. Harry and I heard from a few European friends that they had decided to disembark in Dubai, and we were interested in seeing how many passengers would be left on the ship when we departed Dubai for Africa.

Harry and I avoided discussions with the unhappy passengers as we were quite happy with the change. I was going back to Africa! Ironically, the new itinerary was almost the same as the failed 2022 world cruise. The new itinerary changed the ambiance around the ship. Before, everyone was calm and relaxed, but now, an underlying tension surfaced at unexpected times.

Harry and I shared dinner with friends in the main dining room. Cookie, the maître d, was seating a couple, and the woman started yelling her displeasure about the table and insisting on a different one. Cookie, the sweetest person, selected a second table, and again, the woman got belligerent and started berating Cookie, who then began to cry. The head maître d had to intervene. It was an ugly, unnecessary scene.

The ambiance change may also have been due to human nature. A mass of strangers trapped in a small, enclosed space tends to bring out our worst behavior. There seemed to be more squabbles, tears, and hurt feelings than before the itinerary change. I felt like I was back in high school with cliques and bullying. I hoped things would change as we disembarked passengers in Dubai and moved on to Africa.

CHAPTER 15

Komodo to Taiwan –
Dragons and Cabs

Komodo, Indonesia

KOMODO is one of over seventeen thousand islands that comprise the Republic of Indonesia. It is one of only a handful of islands on which the infamous Komodo Dragon lives. The largest lizard on Earth is named after the main island on which it lives, and it is one of many types of monitor lizards. This was on my bucket list. Since Harry dislikes reptiles, he was happy to stay aboard.

Almost everyone on the ship tendered ashore to participate in the ninety-minute loop around Komodo National Park, a UNESCO World Heritage site. We were searching for free-roaming, fierce, ominous-looking creatures with sharp, saw-like teeth and menacing eyes. We were not allowed to wander alone here but rather we had to stay in our assigned group of twenty with a park guide in the front and back. Both guides carried big sticks as a deterrent in case a dragon was curious or hungry. The dust clung to our sweaty bodies as we wandered through these dry, sparsely vegetated trails in the one-hundred-plus degree heat.

At the start of our walk, our guide was clear that we would stay in a tight-knit group, never wander off the trail, and follow his instructions. Not two minutes into our walk, we saw our first dragon. They were everywhere from three to nine feet and were magnificent creatures. Most of the dragons ignored us, and it was clear that in their minds, we were a nuisance to ignore. But a few of the larger lizards did give us a once over, and I saw intelligence in their eyes. While we walked the loop around several artificial watering holes, I spotted a small species of deer that are the primary food source of these ancient creatures.

At the end of the walk near the "gift shop" with many tee shirts and other souvenir hawkers under their tents, there was a massive dragon. This dragon had a group of people six feet in front of it, but also a group behind, all were taking pictures. It was clear to me that the dragon was on high alert with its head held high, body up off the ground, and feet ready to move. His eyes constantly moved from front to back, looking for a threat or an opportunity for a meal. Who could say which? I started taking my pictures but was distracted by Julia and her husband Ed, fellow passengers, slowly walking backward toward the dragon, taking a selfie. Unbeknownst to them, the dragon was now focused solely on them. They continued to step closer, and the dragon opened its mouth, and the venomous drool started dripping in great strings down to the ground. As they got to within a few feet, I made my angst known by quietly telling them they needed to stop immediately and slowly walk away from the dragon.

It always amazes me how humans disregard the danger that wild animals pose. I have personally seen a parent putting a three-year-old child on the back of a wild bison in Yellowstone so that they can get the perfect picture, a fellow guest in the Galapagos Islands taunting a three-ton bull elephant seal with a red jacket like he was a bullfighter in a ring, and now a woman getting caught up in a selfie. Humans think of ourselves so highly that we disregard animals incorrectly treating them as non-threatening. People get injured or killed because of this mistake. We need to offer these fantastic creatures our respect; they have mine.

Taipei, Taiwan

In my opinion, there is nothing better than a foot massage—soothing, relaxing, and stress-relieving. My solo day did start off that way, but the relaxation effect was short-lived. We drove forty-five minutes by bus into Taipei, a hustling, bustling, busy city. Think of New York with its high rises, remove the cabs and replace them with mopeds and motorbikes in the hundreds of thousands. Nothing like the smell of exhaust in the morning.

On the way to the spa, I was trying to figure out how they would accommodate a busload of people. I was pleasantly surprised. The spa we went to was on several floors, and thirty-two therapists were waiting and ready for our feet. The massage was a full hour, and they added a bonus of neck and shoulders. It was perfect.

Our next stop was the Chiang Kai-shek Memorial Hall. The Taiwanese revere Chiang Kai-shek as a hero who stopped communism and modernized the country. His memorial is an impressive, round, white marble structure in a sixty-two-acre complex. As we got off the bus, we were instructed to be back at the parking space in an hour, and the guide walked us up to the tomb inside the memorial to watch the changing of the guards. After that, I found the gift shop, and with plenty of time to get to the bus, I went shopping. My sense of direction was off because I could not find the bus. I walked about two miles and no bus!

I was late and decided the bus must have already left for our next stop, a famous temple. I decided a cab was the best option, but there could be two problems. The official language of Taiwan is Mandarin Chinese, and I had no local currency. I had a bad feeling about this. The first cab had a driver who did not speak English and would not take credit cards or American cash. I started to get nervous. The second driver saved the day and me. He spoke English, took credit cards, and was a prince among men. I asked him to take me to the famous temple, where we looked for my bus, but it was not there. He was concerned about the bus guide and how we could notify her that I was safe. I had the port agent's local phone number, which SeaSpirit provides at every port for just such issues. This agent could then contact the ship, who could then contact the tour company, who could then contact the guide. He used his phone to call and pass along the message. I suggested he take me back to the ship, a fifty-minute drive. The ride was nerve-racking, as I was lost in a foreign country, trusting a cab driver to take me where I wanted to go. On the route back, I saw several landmarks I had seen on the way, so I felt more at ease. As we approached the ship, I let out my breath and felt extremely lucky it turned out as it did. I was ready for another massage!

CHAPTER 16

Japan to South Korea – Bombs, Chaos and Tea

JAPAN was never on my bucket list. It is a country roughly the size of California with more than three times the population. Due to this dense population and its location and climate, the only wildlife I wanted to see was the Macaque monkeys that lived above the snow line and took baths in the hot springs—my kind of life. So, I was shockingly surprised by the cleanliness of the country and the graciousness of their people to Americans, particularly since we annihilated two of their cities and killed about three hundred and fifty thousand of their citizens during WWII. Nevertheless, I decided to visit Hiroshima.

Hiroshima

The Hiroshima site was designed similarly to Washington DC's Capitol Mall in that it was a long, thin strip of land. The first building at one end is called the Atomic Bomb Dome, which used to house the Prefectural Industrial Promotion Hall. The dome and two sides of the building still stand, but the rest is blackened and full of rubble. It is a symbol of death and destruction. The rest of the site, Hiroshima Peace Park, is all about serenity, reflection, and promoting world peace. At the farthest end of the park is the eternal Flame of Peace that will burn until there is peace throughout the world and there is a commitment to a world without nuclear weapons. Between these two iconic symbols are walkways lined with sweet-smelling cherry blossom trees planted so they bloom all year. Interspersed on the walkways are sculptures designed and donated by world countries to commemorate the wish for peace. The Peace Park touched my heart.

The Hiroshima Peace Memorial Museum is housed in a beautifully modern structure but it was all about devastation. As we made our way into the heart of the museum, they narrowed the huge crowd into small hallways going only in one direction. It felt like a claustrophobic maze to me. I made my way out as quickly as possible, glimpsing photographs of the devastation of the bomb's aftermath. I wish I had stayed outside.

Tokyo

The Luna docked overnight in Tokyo. Harry had his heart set on going to the busiest intersection in the world, the Shibuya Scramble Crossing, with up to three thousand people crossing simultaneously during peak times. It was a nightmare for me as I do not appreciate crowds and get panicky when I do not have enough space around me. I had a slip and fall accident many years ago and need to be able to see every step I take to ensure I do not fall again. But Harry had a burning desire to be a part of the craziness, and he wanted it captured in a video. Since we had free time, we took a cab to the Crossing. We were dropped off a few blocks away, and as we walked toward the Scramble, we saw Luna's captain in the crowd ahead of us. He was not in uniform but at six foot seven inches tall, he was easy to spot in the crowd. We could not catch up with him, even though we did try.

As Harry and I approached the intersection, we saw controlled chaos. It was noisy, with car horns blaring and intense exhaust fumes. We studied the traffic light patterns for a few minutes and then planned the strategy to get a good video of Harry crossing. As I watched the melee, I realized, with some trepidation, that I also wanted to cross. So, after some more planning, we revised our crossing plan to include both of us. Harry was the bravest, so he crossed first, and I captured the moment in a video. Then it was my turn. We both got in position and as the light changed, I tripped as I stepped off the curb. In that split-second, I thought I was a goner, trampled in the busiest intersection in the world; at least I had completed a large part of the circumnavigation of the world, and that would undoubtedly have made a good story. However, in the next instance, I felt a hand on my elbow pulling me upright and whispering for me to walk. So, I walked with the ship's captain at my elbow. He is my hero. And, of course, Harry did a great job of capturing it all. A bit of drama, with most of the trauma avoided except for my bruised ego!

Seoul, South Korea

I never in my wildest dreams thought I would be privileged to go to South Korea. When I started thinking about a world cruise more than twenty years ago, this country was not open to tourism, and its proximity to North Korea was scary to me. However, I was not going to pass up the opportunity. Harry and I hopped on a bus to Hoenbeopsa Temple, a Buddhist temple high in the hills with blooming cherry blossom trees. The temple is in the traditional cake style, with each floor smaller than the one below. The hand-painted detail and intricate blue, green, and red ornamentation on the temple's exterior were exquisite.

The "Darye" tea ceremony has been practiced for thousands of years here. During the elegant ceremony, we learned many of the ritual's nuances, including visual beauty, the aroma of the tea, and its flavor. The experience is intended to heighten the senses and provide a path to spiritual enlightenment. It was held in a special room where we were required to remove our shoes. Harry elected to sit in the traditional manner on a pillow on the floor with tea paraphernalia on a tiny table. I elected to sit in a chair at a Western-style table. We were supposed to find a partner as you would participate in the tea making. I was the odd girl out, so one of the women who facilitated the ceremony offered her shy nine-year-old daughter, who was apprenticing to be a facilitator. All the women wore traditional Korean outfits: a long skirt with a white under blouse covered by a cropped jacket tied with ribbons. The whole outfit was made of stiff fabric like thick chiffon, all in pastel colors. They were stunning.

The mistress of the ceremony (a retired university professor of the Tea Ceremony) spoke in Korean, and our guide translated the steps for preparing the tea. As this temple is a "meditation" temple, we started and ended the ceremony with a few minutes of reflection. Each part of the tea-making process was exacting, from warming the teapot and cup with hot water to adding the proper amount of green tea leaves. The ceremony took about forty-five minutes. Most of the people sitting on the floor got quite uncomfortable. Harry's partner had to move to a higher table before the ceremony was done. On the other hand, Harry was straight-backed, cross-legged, and serene until it was time to leave. He would be a great model for a Buddha statue.

Our last stop was at the Jagalchi Fish Market, the sixth-largest fish market in the world. If you have ever been to Seattle's Pike's Place Fish Market, where they throw fish in the air, think something larger. The entire market of Pike's Place could fit into this fish market ten times. Outside vendors sell dried products like starfish, seaweed, and salted cod. The market's second floor has restaurants where you can take your purchased fish and have them cook it any way you wish while you wait. However, the real show is inside this vast warehouse where the live products are sold chiefly by middle-aged women, as is tradition. As we approached the building, we started to hear the calls of fishmongers, and then we caught the scent in the air. As we entered the building, the sound of running water joined the cacophony of voices. Each of the many aisles had drainage grates below to catch the runoff from the fish tanks where every type of sea creature was held. Anything from the tiniest shrimp to a one-hundred-pound tuna could be found here. The tanks held sea horses, clams, oysters, and shellfish. There were fish species too numerous to count and some that I had never seen before. It was fascinating and overwhelming all at the same time. If I were to choose my dinner, I would have to pick the cold-water lobsters, but the colossal shrimp were a second choice as I have never seen shrimp that big. I thought about returning to the Luna and asking the chef to cook some for me. I am unsure what that outcome would have been.

Japan and Seoul were pleasant surprises on my journey. I have never been in a country as clean as Japan, and the citizens were helpful and courteous. In my previous travels, my encounters with Asians have been anything but smooth. I found them to be rude and pushy. In my mind, it had to do with the high-density population needing to fight for space. After my time in Japan, it became obvious that this is not a Japanese trait.

CHAPTER 17

Shanghai and Overland China – Speed, Crowds and Control

C HINA is huge, and its cities are overpopulated. Massive crowds were the norm everywhere we went, but China, being technologically advanced, used these tools to make processes more streamlined. China required us to carry our passports. In most other countries, they stayed in the ship's purser's office. Our passports were used as tickets to get into most venues via their sophisticated reservation system, and in airports and train stations, facial recognition was used for the same purpose. The contrast between the highly advanced, technologically savvy country and the street sweepers, older adults using handmade twig brooms, was mindboggling.

Shanghai

Harry and I were looking forward to riding the fastest train in the world. The Maglev train has no wheels, floats on an electromagnetic cushion, can race along a guideway at speeds of up to one hundred and eighty-six mph, and has a max speed of two hundred and sixty-seven mph. It took two minutes to get to one hundred and eighty-six mph and another two minutes to slow back to zero. The ride was too short as we did the round-trip journey from the city to the airport in eight minutes each way. The ride by car in regular traffic is over an hour.

Overland China

Harry and I chose the same overland experience, covering all the major landmarks with one exception. I had always wanted to see the giant pandas in the Wolong Research Center, one of the few places in the world successfully breeding pandas and repopulating the species into the wild. Pandas are one of the most endangered species. Ten years ago, I watched an episode of "60 Minutes," they did a story on these fascinating animals and spent most of the time in this research center. They showed the opening of the doors to the facility in the morning and huge crowds streaming in with over twenty thousand visitors a day. The viewing areas had six people deep trying to get a glimpse of these magnificent creatures. I decided then that I would skip seeing the pandas, but I am glad they are working to keep the population from going extinct.

Beijing, Overland Day One

Beijing's architecture is totally different from Shanghai's. Shanghai is more modern, representing the future, while Beijing has all concrete square buildings representing the present. Xi'an's architecture is ancient history.

Our first stop was the Temple of Heaven, a complex of religious buildings constructed during the Ming Dynasty in the early fifteenth century. The most prominent building is the Hall of Prayer for Good Harvests, a circular structure with a blue roof. It is proof of the superstitiousness of these people and reflects symbolism and numerology in its design. Today, the Temple of Heaven remains an important cultural and historical site, attracting millions of visitors annually. I think they all arrived the day we did! The emperor was considered the people's conduit to God. This temple depicts this with the three roof levels: God, the emperor, and the people. The emperor would go twice yearly to the temple, once before and once after the harvest.

The day we were there, we had to wait in a very, very, very long line as about three hundred thousand people visit this site every day! It was not a single line like at Disney, but a line a dozen people wide. We were funneled through an open-air passageway. I had to make my way to the outermost line so I could breathe, trying to ignore the thousands of people enclosing me in a small space.

As we wandered around this complex, marveling at these ancient buildings, I noticed young teenage girls walking around and posing in traditional dress with a camera crew in tow. Families bring their daughters to the temple grounds, rent wigs and costumes for a hefty sum, and believe that these pictures will bring prosperity and good luck. China was a country that murdered their daughters at birth since they had no value to the family as breadwinners. Quite the contrast.

Our next stop was the infamous Tiananmen Square, the largest public square in the world at one hundred and nine acres, which can hold at least one million people. It is one of China's most iconic and historically significant public spaces. We were forewarned about asking questions or discussing politics in public before we disembarked from our bus for the long walk to the square. We could discuss these things on the bus, but nowhere else. Big Brother was watching and listening; freedom of speech does not exist here.

Tiananmen Square has played a crucial role in China's modern history. It has been the site of numerous important events and political demonstrations, both peaceful and tumultuous, that have significantly shaped the nation's course. Various national monuments and buildings flank the square, including the Gate of Heavenly Purity, the National Museum of China, and the Great Hall of the People to name a few. At the square's southern end is a large portrait of Mao Zedong, the founding father of the People's Republic of China. The picture is displayed above the entrance to the Forbidden City and is a prominent symbol of the Chinese Communist Party.

In 1919, Tiananmen Square was a focal point for the May Fourth Movement, a student-led protest against the Chinese government's response to the Treaty of Versailles, which ceded Chinese territories to Japan following World War I. In recent history, the most well-known and controversial event associated with the square is the 1989 pro-democracy protests. Many will remember the man who stood up to a Chinese tank, sparking the protest of tens of thousands of students and citizens who gathered in the square to demand political and economic reforms. The government declared martial law and ordered a military crackdown that resulted in the loss of many lives. The exact number is disputed. China has said there are no more than three hundred, but the Red Cross has estimated that it is up to one thousand. The Chinese government considers these events taboo and tightly controls discussions and information related to the incident.

Our accommodation for the night was the Beijing Sheraton, which was upscale; it would have fit easily in New York City and had all the bells and whistles; I am not sure about listening devices. We were on our own for dinner, and after walking five miles during the day, I was starving and wanted to avoid walking anywhere, so we took the elevator up to their onsite Japanese Italian restaurant. The language issue made ordering difficult, but the manager spoke English, and we had seafood. I was hoping for Peking Duck, but that was not available.

Beijing, Overland Day Two

The Forbidden City, also known as the Imperial Palace, is a historic complex located in the heart of the city. It was built between 1406 and 1420 and was the home of the emperors of the Ming and Qing dynasties for nearly 500 years, ending in 1912, when the last dynasty fell. It serves as the political and ceremonial center of the Chinese government.

The Forbidden City is renowned for its splendid and well-preserved traditional Chinese architecture. It comprises nine hundred and eighty surviving buildings with just under ten thousand rooms, all adorned with intricate wooden carvings, colorful roof tiles, and exquisite artwork. The layout of the complex adheres to the principles of feng shui and is considered a masterpiece of traditional Chinese architecture. Each building has a balanced counterpart, such as water and fire. Every building has an odd number of dragons on the roof. The lowest number of dragons means the building is not as important. The highest number, nine, was thought to bring luck. Today, the Chinese believe the lucky number is eight since the Chinese word for prosperity sounds like eight. They all want license plates and cell phone numbers to have lots of eights. The Chinese are and always have been a superstitious lot.

The name "Forbidden City" was a place where access was strictly controlled, and ordinary citizens were not allowed to enter without permission. Only the emperor, his family, and select officials were permitted inside. The Forbidden City was designated a UNESCO World Heritage site and is recognized as one of the world's most important cultural and historical sites. The city itself is massive, with an outer courtyard where the emperor held court doing the business of the empire. The inner court was to take care of his needs and the needs of many concubines and children.

Remarkably, these ancient buildings are well-preserved and revered in today's modern world. In comparison, the United States is an infant, and we think our historic sites from the 1700s are old.

The Great Wall, Overland Day Two

The Great Wall of China is one of the most iconic landmarks in the world. It was built over centuries to protect against invasions by various nomadic tribes. The wall stretches over thirteen thousand miles. The section of the wall we went to is only eight hundred years old. The oldest section is about twenty-two hundred years old. I am not a mountain goat. Harry is more of a mountain goat than me, but the stairs are eight hundred years old and worn. They are uneven and ragged; some are equivalent in height to three of our typical steps. We did, however, walk on the Great Wall of China; how amazing! I did about ten stairs, and Harry did a few hundred.

Xi'an, Overland Day Three

The Terracotta Army Museum site is one of the most significant archaeological discoveries in the world and a UNESCO World Heritage site. The Terracotta Army was discovered in 1974 by local farmers digging a well near Xi'an. Qin Shi Huang, China's first emperor, created the Terracotta Army, established the Qin Dynasty, and united China. He ordered the construction of the Terracotta Army to serve as his guardians in the afterlife. It includes eight thousand life-sized clay sculptures, including soldiers, horses, chariots, and other military figures, but many parts of the site remain unexcavated. One of the most remarkable aspects of the army is that each soldier appears to be unique. The statues are meticulously detailed, with distinct facial features, hairstyles, and clothing befitting military rank. The army was initially brightly painted, but over time, the colors faded. The challenge of preserving the paint and preventing further fading is an ongoing concern for archaeologists and conservationists.

In most burial sites, any accompanied persons would have been killed or buried alive with the deceased. This emperor must have had a lot of enemies to have seen a need to create such a vast army.

As I expected, this trip was exhausting. We walked more than five miles daily, and each day started early in the morning and ended well past dark. The trip was well worth it, but China is a been there and done that place for me. It had been on my bucket list for years, and this being my third attempt to get there, I was happy I finally made it.

CHAPTER 18

Vietnam

I HAD mixed feelings about going to Vietnam as it is a communist country, and we fought a bloody war there, unsuccessfully. I knew boys who had fought there and came home to no welcoming committee. I remember the news reports when I was in my teens about the death and destruction, but I had been hearing wonderful things about the country for a few years from travel enthusiasts, so I was optimistic. I chose a mix of excursions that were historical or nature driven.

Hanoi

Interestingly, our first port of call was in Hanoi at the northern end of Vietnam. Ideologically, the communist end of the country. As we moved south to other Vietnamese ports, the demeanor, and interactions with the people changed as we moved further away from the center of government. It was remarkable that you could sense freedom the further South we traveled. Of course, this was in the hearts and minds of those in the South. It was clear that the reunification to one government did not influence what was in the hearts of the people. The South Vietnamese sounded and acted freer.

Hanoi is a thriving, overcrowded city with motorbikes, thousands and thousands of motorbikes, but not many cars. Every time we left the bus, "big brother," men in dark suits using in-ear monitors and walkie-talkies were clearly watching us and our guide closely. There was military everywhere and we were warned never to take their picture. While on the bus, the guide made it clear that all political questions or discussions with him needed to take place on the bus. Nothing was to be said while on the street or in historical sites. In the North, to get a job, stay in a job, get into a good school, and move ahead, you need money because there is flagrant corruption. Every year, gifts, preferably cash, must be given to your boss for births, birthdays, deaths, and major holidays, or you would be replaced!

Our first stop was at the infamous Hoa Lo prison, the Hanoi Hilton, in the heart of the walled city. This prison was used first by the French to imprison Vietnamese dissidents and, during the Vietnam War, to hold American pilots, including John McCain. It was grim, but the guide said the conditions were not so harsh for the Americans, and we all know differently.

After leaving the prison, we went to the Temple of Literature, another historical highlight, as it was constructed as a university in 1070 to honor Confucius. It was where the sons of kings and the privileged were taught. We then moved on to the Ho Chi Minh Mausoleum. The people revere Ho Chi Minh as he brought independence to Vietnam. Big brother was in clear evidence here paying close attention to everything the guide had to say. And based on his tone and demeanor, I understood he was reciting the pre-approved script.

Ha Long Bay

Ha Long Bay, located in northeastern Vietnam, is a UNESCO World Heritage site and one of the country's most iconic and breathtaking natural wonders. It is renowned for its stunning limestone formations and emerald-green waters that inspired the set design of the movie Avatar. As the junk (boat) cruised through the bay, we both marveled at this natural work of art, with thousands of limestone islets soaring dramatically from the waters.

Saigon

Our first stop involved transferring to a sampan boat that took us on the Mekong River delta to Unicorn Island. The Mekong River starts high in the Himalayas and flows all the way down to its exit into the South China Sea. Due to the large amount of silt going down river, the delta is fertile and produces rice to feed the Vietnamese and for export. This country is the number two rice producer in the world.

We wandered around a residential-commercial farming area until we came upon a dock where many four-person traditional canoes were waiting with a paddler on the gunwale at the stern. We were each handed a traditional conical bamboo hat to put on. We got situated in these wobbly canoes for a ten-minute canoe ride down this narrow canal. The water was grey, and the canal's banks were grey from the silt in the delta. The air smelled earthy and fetid. There were some plants that I had never seen before, but this might be because they were all grey, and I did not recognize them due to their coloring. The crazy Vietnamese woman paddling our canoe kept trying to pass other boats to get us down the canal more quickly and kept saying "tip, tip." The canoe was unstable, and I had visions of us capsizing and having to crawl to shore. Ultimately, she dumped us onto the far dock, but not before we gave her the tip she insisted on. I would not want to repeat this excursion.

Vietnam was a place of beauty with a brutal history. I am glad I toured it and just as glad to move on.

CHAPTER 19

Singapore – Gardens, Lights and Slings

I HAD no preconceived notions about Singapore before this trip, except I had heard through friends that it was safe, young, and cosmopolitan, all of which are true. Singapore is a sovereign city-state in Malaysia that is one degree north of the equator, so as expected, it was extremely hot and humid. The island of Singapore started as a small fishing village with a natural deep-water harbor. It had one hundred and fifty residents when Stamford Raffles traveled there for the spices, which were literally worth their weight in gold. The French, Dutch, English, and Portuguese had come before him, but he saw the promise of a port here. He signed a treaty with the local Malays and made it a free port with no taxes to enter, so this brought all the traders to Singapore rather than other ports in the region. With all the trade, workers were needed, which brought Chinese and Indian workers here. Three years after signing the treaty, the population rose to ten thousand. Two hundred and five years later, the island is physically twenty-five percent larger due to land reclamation.

Politically, the government rules via stringent regulations and severe penalties if not followed. All people are categorized by ethnicity, and the government is working on complete assimilation based on population percentages. Seventy percent of the population is Chinese, and housing is allocated based on that percentage. You cannot own an apartment in a building if the ethnicity numbers are incorrect. English is the first language for all in school, and everyone takes a second language based on ethnicity.

This small island revers green space and has three hundred parks. A fifty-year plan guides all growth for infrastructure and building, which started in 1961. They are in the planning stages for the next fifty years. The infrastructure is underground for water, cabling, electricity, transit, and sewage. Only ten percent of people are allowed to have cars, and every month, as someone gives up a car, that certificate is transferred via lottery. Between the cost of the vehicle, say a forty-five thousand dollars Toyota Corolla, and the money you pay for the ten-year certificate, ninety-five thousand dollars, you pay one hundred and fifty thousand dollars for that car.

As we had two days here, we both chose to spend the first day on a tour to see the highlights and left the second day for us to explore on our own. Our first stop on day one was the National Orchid Garden. This garden is a UNESCO World Heritage site, and if I lived here, I would have a yearly pass. I could never have enough time here. There were so many gorgeous orchids in this garden. I have never seen so many in one place. Everywhere you looked, there were blooming, colorful, bright, and vibrant orchids of every variety. The garden was exquisitely designed with wandering paths bordered with flowers and sometimes overhung with blooms. About halfway through our time here, I spotted a worker removing dead or dying leaves from the plants with a pair of kitchen tongs, one leaf at a time. No wonder I did not see a single plant with a brown leaf or a wilting flower anywhere.

From the orchid garden, we were off to Esplanade Park, where the famous Merlion statue, an iconic Singapore landmark, resides. It is half lion and half mermaid and all about whimsey, not inspired by any legend or fable. It sits on the edge of a small lagoon where several iconic buildings can be viewed. The Marina Bay Sands Hotel consists of three towers with what appears to be a ship on top. Next to it is a building designed to look like a lotus flower, which houses the ArtScience museum. At night, the lagoon transforms into a theater, home to the hotel's light show.

That evening, we took the subway to the Raffles Hotel. I was nervous, but we were with a group of friends who had traveled the subway before. The tunnels and trains were so clean that the two-second rule would be acceptable here—that would not be acceptable anywhere in the United States. There was also no rushing, shoving, or pushing, it seemed I was in a false reality.

Raffles is the home of the Singapore Sling. Ladies in the early years got bored of drinking tea in the afternoon, so this drink was created as an alternative. It is made with gin, brandy, grenadine, bitters, lime, and pineapple juice and it is delicious. Everyone goes to the Long Bar in the hotel, and we were no exception. We all ordered a Sling. The drinks were twenty-six dollars each and came with a bag of peanuts. The waitress indicated the shells were to be discarded on the floor. We complied.

From Raffles, we headed back to Esplanade Park to see the light show and then took a cab back to the ship. It was a great, tiring, five-mile day.

I wanted to go to the digital art museum when we were in Tokyo. We could not get tickets online, so I suggested we go there anyway and see if we could get in. I begged the young girl at the entrance, but my pleas went on deaf ears. After researching, I learned that the same company had an installation in Singapore, so we pre-purchased tickets for the morning of our second day here. We took a cab over to the Lotus which we had seen the day before, and the lily pond surrounding the museum was full of lotus flowers.

The art displays were all digital. As we moved through each room, we viewed and walked among interactive art on the walls and the floor. My favorite room was breathtaking and scary at the same time. The room was hung with light strips that changed colors and design as you moved through it. You were required to walk on a designated path through the light strings. The floor, which was not on the path, was mirrored, so it appeared like you would fall off the path into an abyss. I was petrified I was going to drop into the black hole. I took baby steps through the exhibit and would not let go of Harry's arm. We both loved the experience, and it was well worth the wait.

Our last stop in Singapore was to a place on my bucket list, the massive Gardens by the Bay. It is home to iconic purple tree sculptures and several buildings. It is an amusement area for adults; kids are allowed, but there are no rides here. As we were running out of time, we chose to go to Mist House because we suspected it would be cooler on this one-hundred-plus-degree day, and it was. It is a garden in a seven-story glass building with a waterfall inside. We took the elevator to the top of the building and walked the spiral pathways around the waterfall down through the flower-lined paths to the bottom. It was another five-mile day, and I could not wait to return to the ship for a good soak in the pool, but it was terrific. Two days in Singapore was not enough.

Harry and I would love to return to Singapore someday, but it is a country of contrasts. It is tourist-friendly, everyone speaks English, and credit cards are accepted everywhere. It is technologically progressive, but it is not a democracy. The government rules with an iron fist. There are many signs of what not to do. Caning is used as punishment here. It's not something I, for one, would want to experience. Spitting and gum chewing are just two things you could get caned for. This deterrent does seem to have the effect the government wants. The streets are clean; the people are friendly and well-mannered. It is an interesting society where we do not wish to live but would visit again when the weather is cooler and the humidity is gone if that ever happens.

CHAPTER 20

On Personal Care

MY haircuts on the ship were problematic; Harry never had an issue. My hair has been worn short since college. I have never been good at styling and never wanted to spend the time every day. I towel it dry and brush through it to get the natural curl and waves to show themselves. My hair needs cutting every five weeks, so I knew there would be at least four appointments with the hairdresser in the spa. My first cut was with a gentleman I nicknamed Edward Scissorhands. I had the fastest haircut ever. It usually takes no more than twenty minutes for me to get a haircut, but with Edward, I was done and out the door in ten. And it was perfect! I felt good about future cuts. I should have known better.

The second cut was with a new crew member. She was suitable for men but did not know what a quarter of an inch meant. She cut my hair too short. The third cut was also with her, and I told her not to cut it too short, but she kept cutting to even up the sides. She went back and forth a few times, and it got shorter and shorter. I finally stopped her mid-cut and said, "Enough." I have never been one to angst over my hair as it grows way too quickly and knew it would grow back soon.

I hoped I would return home before needing another cut, but I could not wait that long. I complained to my trivia team member Gladys, who has terrific curly short hair. I mentioned, "I did not want to return to the spa." She told me that "she cuts her hair, and she would gladly do mine." I heartily agreed, but it turns out she did not have the proper tools. I returned to my cabin to get my scissors, which worked well for most of it. I have a long hairline, as she does, and she was using her husband's electric razor to clean up the back. When she was ready to start the back of my head, she plugged it in, and it was dead. I was unsure what her husband would use as a shaver for the rest of the voyage. When we finished, it was better than going to the spa, and I could survive until I made it back home. Thank goodness for Gladys.

CHAPTER 21

Malaysia – Apes and Timing

P ENANG is a Malaysian state that was once part of the British Empire. Today, it is ruled by five sultans who inherit their titles. Every five years, the five sultans elect a king who has the ultimate power. There are just under two million residents in this crowded, bustling capital city.

When I first chose this voyage and saw Borneo on the itinerary, I knew I needed to see orangutans, preferably at the Sepilok Orangutan Rehabilitation Center in Sandakan, Malaysia, a city on the island of Borneo. The ship docked in Kota Kinabalu on the opposite side of the island. It was a seven-hour drive or a twenty-minute flight away, but flights were only twice a week. I spent hours trying to find a way to get across the island without missing the ship. Harry was not interested. I was willing to spend a night there and meet the ship at the next port of call, but I could find no way to accomplish this where I would be secure in getting back to the ship on time and safely. I gave up, only to go through the same exercise a few months later, when I finally gave up for good. And then miraculously, a few months before we set sail from Los Angeles, I spoke with another world traveler, and she told me about an orangutan sanctuary in Penang, Malaysia, a port we would be visiting. After more planning, I secured a local guide to take me there and to see some of the city. Before leaving home, I put my private excursion details on the SeaSpirit messaging site, and three couples, including Gladys and Lincoln, agreed to join me. It was a win-win.

We all met in the theater and then headed with our private guide to Orang Utan Island, off the mainland of Malaysia. Yes, that's not a typo. "Orangutan" is the English version of the Malay words "Orang" and "Utan," which translates to "Jungle Man." The Bukit Merah Orang Utan Island Foundation operates a rehabilitation center on a thirty-five-acre island founded in 2000. There are three orangutan species, all of which have extremely low reproductive rates in the wild, making them highly endangered. Thirty thousand Bornean Orangutans are left in the wild, six thousand Sumatran, and only about six hundred of the newly discovered Tapanuli species. The orangutans in the center live in natural surroundings instead of cages with dedicated staff to care for them. There is also a nursery and research center for orangutans on the property. For the tour, the visitors walk through a covered mesh-fenced walkway. We humans were in a cage; the orangutans roamed free.

Orangutans are brought to the island if injured, orphaned, or caught in an animal trafficking scheme. There were thirty-four apes here once; there were only fourteen when we arrived. Most were born on the island or unable to return to the wild. There is a second island across the bay where they pre-release orangutans that may be ready to return to the wild. If they thrive there, they can be re-introduced to the wild. Unfortunately, there were no apes on that island, but to date, they have cared for twenty orangutans and released fourteen.

We took a ferry from the city pier to the island, and the heat and humidity were oppressive. We knew there would be no air conditioning in the jungle where we were going; all we could hope for was shade or a breeze. There was neither. As we approached the dock on the island, we saw a lush jungle behind the information center and gift shop. As we walked through to the entrance, there was a life-size wooden orangutan statue to greet us. It was so much bigger than I expected and intimidating. A few more steps later, we were outside and saw a big male having breakfast in the lagoon under a feeding platform. He seemed wise to me in the shade and in the water. It's the coolest place around. He had dark fleshy cheek pads only seen on males and was covered with bright orange hair. He was amazing to see. Orangutans do not swim, which is why sanctuaries are all on islands. I was surprised to see one in the water. They like water but will only go in if their feet are secure on the bottom or they have a tree to hold on to.

The entire walkway was double fenced on both sides and above us. These animals must have limited human contact to be released into the wild. We could watch and drop apples into some tubes for them, but no other contact was allowed. Some females huddled around the tubes as we wandered through this tunnel, expecting apples to supplement their breakfast. The center had set up a jungle gym, and to my great surprise and pleasure, there was a baby who was straying away from her mother. This one was full of curiosity and bravado, and it left Mom, walked over to the jungle gym, scurried up a thick rope, and started to swing and climb up to the top. When she arrived, she glanced at her mom as if to say, "Hey, look at me; I am smart and courageous!" We stayed as long as we could tolerate, as the heat and sun were brutal.

We stopped at a local market so Gladys could buy additional suitcases to hold gifts for all their grandchildren. As she was shopping, I was getting nervous as it was fast approaching the deadline to return to the Luna. When we were finally on our way to the ship with sufficient time, we got in a traffic jam. We had no option but to make the painful crawl to the port. We were going to be late.

I was trying not to panic, as it was all out of my control. When we made it through port security and around a series of three-story warehouses, we could finally see the Luna with her gangway down and crew getting ready to remove it. They saw us approach and stopped what they were doing until we all walked up the gangway. Phew! I could breathe again. We were the last to arrive, and Paulina was waiting for us on the red carpet, looking very stern. She made clear to us the captain's displeasure at holding up departure. She told us, "Two minutes and we would have been left behind," a terrifying thought. Barring all that, it was another fantastic day, enjoying the natural world.

CHAPTER 22

Thailand and Sri Lanka – Flowers, Parlors and Elephants

I DID not know enough about Thailand. I did know that Thai people were lovely, that Thai food, specifically Pad Thai, was delicious. I knew that the people are predominantly Buddhist, that the country used to be called Siam and was noted for having the best rubies in the world. I knew that it was very hot and was famous for their massages. But that was all I knew, which was nowhere near enough.

Bangkok

The Bangkok Flower Market is breathtaking. Being that I adore flowers and orchids, I was mesmerized. As we wove down long corridors in a vast warehouse, the colors and smells were awe-inspiring. There were hundreds of different varieties of flowers, such as jasmine, orchids of all kinds, and chrysanthemums, all ridiculously inexpensive. I did not have enough time here as there was no time to shop. Maybe that was a good thing, deciding what to take back to the ship would have been daunting. Someone quickly bought a gallon bag full of orchid stems for about three dollars. These would have cost a hundred or more in America.

After leaving the market, we hopped into a tuk-tuk, a three-wheeled motorized vehicle. The driver was in front, and Harry and I were in the back. It was all open to the nice breeze with exhaust fumes all around. There was a cover for shade, which was helpful as it was one hundred and seven degrees. As we made our way to our next stop, our driver recklessly swerved around cars, buses, and waves of motorcycles and pushed carts. As you might expect, I was holding on tight, and Harry smiled from ear to ear. The final stop was to the reclining Buddha.

We saw hundreds of Buddha statues in many countries on this world adventure. Buddha is considered a God and can manifest itself in many different forms as interpreted by the artist. We saw a Buddha with red lipstick and earrings, some in jade, some covered with gold leaf, some in the lotus position, some small enough to fit in the palm of my hand, and some inspiringly large. We saw the reclining Buddha depicting the state of nirvana, one hundred and sixty feet long and covered in gold paint. We also went to a temple where three walls were covered in tiny alcoves, each with its statue of Buddha representing a different manifestation. There were hundreds and hundreds. It was interesting that while visiting these Buddhas, I never got a sense of serenity and calmness that always affects me when I enter a Christian church, a Shinto shrine, or a Jewish temple. There were always lots of people around hurriedly giving offerings of flowers or money. It was never peaceful or reflexive.

During the short walk through a small green park on our way to see the reclining Buddha, I saw what appeared to be an older woman dressed in a long, traditional black dress. I had spotted her because she was standing behind a two-foot by two-foot cage full of small brown sparrow-like birds. There were at least one hundred in this filthy cage, all squawking as if to say, "Let me out of here, now." My heart broke for them. I took our guide over to her to translate for me, and he was helpful. He told me that she would release a bird for one dollar and that releasing them at the temple brings good fortune to the person putting up the cash. I was livid; making these tiny creatures suffer for superstitions was criminal in my mind. I took out my money and told her that I would give her the cash if she released them all. She reached into the cage and grabbed a bird one by one, setting it free until no birds were left. I knew she would be back tomorrow with another cage full, but at least these birds could fly free.

Koh Samui

Koh Samui is a small port, and none of the SeaSpirit excursions held any interest. I am sure you have all heard of the famous (or infamous) Thailand massages; I wanted to try them. When I got off the ship's tender onto the dock, I walked two blocks uphill to the main town, which was three blocks square. I walked around the area to get the lay of the land, and to my happy surprise, there were five different massage parlors. I was concerned about having only U.S. dollars or plastic, but I remained optimistic that one of these places would have what I wanted. The windows were obscured at every parlor, and shoes were outside, a custom I did not expect. I went to my first choice and off went the sneakers and socks. I walked into a clean salon that looked like a mani-pedi shop. I assumed that the massage beds were in the back. I told the receptionist what I was searching for, and she indicated that they had no available appointments. I went back outside and donned my shoes and socks. Now I understood why every parlor had a seat of some sort at the door.

I walked a few stores up the street to my number two choice. Off went my shoes and socks, and I went in and was told there was no available space. All the pedicure chairs were full. On my third attempt, I had learned to stick my head inside and ask about availability before I took my shoes and socks off. I was down to the last parlor and was not optimistic until I saw only one pair of shoes outside. When I stuck my head in, a lone woman was in a chair, and several Thai women were waiting for customers. I do not go into restaurants that have only a few cars outside. It is a clear sign that there might be a problem with the food or the service. But I was out of options, so I went when the receptionist waved me in.

As I tried to articulate what services I wanted, it was clear English was not well understood here. I gestured as well as I could, and she seemed to understand, but I forgot to ask about currency. I was shown a pedicure chair, and she indicated I should sit. My original intent was a hand and foot massage. I had heard all about happy endings in Thai massage parlors, and that was not what I had in mind, so I opted for a fully clothed hand and foot massage, and because of the language issues, I opted for a mani-pedi as well.

I had the most relaxing manicure/pedicure for two hours and then a foot and hand massage. I was in heaven, except about halfway through the process, I remembered about the possible currency issue. What would I do if they only took Thai Baht? I thought I could find an ATM in town but was concerned. I should not have worried; they took plastic, and thirty dollars later, with a bottle of virgin coconut oil, I was on my way, putting my shoes and socks back on. (The cost on the ship would have been a minimum of four hundred dollars).

My other goal for my day in Ko Samui was to have Pad Thai in Thailand. It is one of my favorite foods. I had seen an outside restaurant before the pier, so I walked over. It was another one-hundred-plus-degree day, but the place did have fans, so I thought I would be okay. I determined that the owner did speak a little English and would take a credit card. I ordered mild shrimp, chicken Pad Thai, and a mango smoothie. While I waited for my food to be cooked in a wok at the entrance to the restaurant, I saw many crew from the Luna coming and going from the ship. Everyone had a haircut. I wish I had known that a few days earlier.

The food came with the Pad Thai on a green plate with a banana leaf underneath. I first saw an ant walking across the plate and three undercooked shrimp. On closer inspection, I saw a second ant, which I squished with my finger. I have been warned never to eat street food when traveling and have seen disaster strike others, so I was cautious as I proceeded to take a taste. It was delicious, and I saw two more ants. I determined they were coming from the banana leaf, not the food. So, I finished the Pad Thai without eating the shrimp. The owner asked if I wanted the shrimp re-cooked as they traditionally eat them undercooked. I refused and paid the five dollars I owed! Thankfully, there were no consequences from eating street food.

Phuket

Elephants and Thai culture are deeply intertwined. In the country, elephants are sacred and thought to bring good fortune and prosperity. Not too long ago, they were enslaved for logging, warfare, and transportation. Today, the relationship between elephants and the Thai people has evolved, focusing on conservation and awareness. Elephants are still used in ceremonies, and many are housed in sanctuaries, protecting the species and bringing in the dollars to pay for their upkeep.

My first encounter with Asian elephants was in a privately owned camp outside of Phuket that housed nine rescued elephants due to mistreatment or illegal trade. All were purchased, and the camp depends on the donations to sustain it. All the elephants here are female, as they are less aggressive and can safely interact with the public. They will spend the rest of their long lives here.

When I arrived, they gave me a bowl filled with vitamins, grains, bananas, and other ingredients, a bucket, and one glove. I was shown how to mix all the ingredients into a "vitamin ball," which I put in my bucket, with sugar cane stalks and more bananas. By this time, my clothes were soaked with sweat, which was helpful, as I had a magic towel. A chemical reaction occurs when you wet the towel, causing the towel to cool. Since no water was available, I kept using my sweat to cool the towel. It was helpful, wiping away the sweat and cooling me slightly.

I then headed off to the elephant "dining room," a dusty area with thatched awnings to shade the elephants. It was again one hundred and seven plus degrees. I chose a medium-sized adult (not too intimidating), and she was ready for breakfast. Asian elephants are smaller than their African cousins, but she was about eight feet tall and weighed five thousand pounds. All these elephants had distinct personalities and preferences. Some wanted bananas before sugar cane, and others wanted their vitamins. They were also not shy about letting you know their preference. They either took what you offered, dropped it, or reached into the bucket to take what they wanted. They reminded me of toddlers who were picky eaters. We were not given any restrictions on how to interact with them. As the mahout (handler) took my picture with my chosen elephant, the elephant wrapped its trunk around my body and pulled me in for a hug. At first, I was unsure what she was doing, but she made it clear it was a hug, and I was pleasantly surprised. Their skin is soft, but their heads are covered with short, bristly hair.

After breakfast, it was bathing time. All the elephants, led by their mahouts, walked down to the watering hole for a cooling bath, which seemed to make them very happy. They flapped their ears and sprayed themselves and everyone around them with water, including me. We then all moved on to the mud hole, where they used the mud as a bug repellent, parasite removal system, and suntan lotion.

It was a great day, one I will cherish forever, as I got a hug from an elephant. What could be better than that?

Pinnawala, Sri Lanka

You can never get enough elephants, so I elected to see more and went to the Pinnawala Elephant Orphanage and Conservation Center. The group boarded a bus for the two-hour ride through the city and into the lush countryside. Where Phuket was dry and dusty, this area was green but just as hot.

Pinnawala cares for motherless baby elephants and rehabilitates injured elephants; they house over eighty. The orphanage has the rare distinction of successfully breeding elephants in captivity, further protecting the species. They also have twin babies, which is highly unusual for elephants. We arrived at the center before ten in the morning and saw the elephants leaving their home and walking across the street down to the river, dodging souvenir stalls on either side. We were close enough to touch them, but these elephants are considered wild, so touching was ill-advised.

There were babies, females, and very large males wearing heavy chains to keep them under control, but they were not tied together, so any one of them could have walked away. These elephants had exceptionally dark skin, and at first, I thought they were covered by mud, but that was not the case. The Sri Lankan Asian sub-species are the darkest of all the elephant species.

We watched the elephants enjoying a cool down and soaking in the river from the lovely balconies of our lunch venue. The mahouts were splashing them with colossal water cannons, and some wallowed in the shallows. My eyes gravitated to an old, large male. He had found his spot in the river and slowly lowered himself so that he was submerged. Only the tip of his trunk was exposed, like a snorkel, so that he could breathe. He was taking his massive weight off his old bones and enjoying the day. I could relate. The river was his Thalassotherapy pool.

After lunch, we followed the elephants back across the street, again avoiding all the street vendors, to their home, where we had the opportunity to help feed them and watch them intermingle. It was a hot and long day like yesterday, but it was worth the effort!

I loved this part of the world and could see myself coming back here.

CHAPTER 23

India – No Lions, But Tigers and Bears, Oh My

I WAS very conflicted when Harry and I got the list of available overland tours, including the Taj Mahal, Napal, and Tigers, and Pink City. I wanted to do all three, but since they all left and returned the same day, I had to make a choice. As we have already established, I am all about wildlife; I chose the Tigers. Harry went to the Taj Mahal.

The Bengal tiger, found primarily in India, is highly endangered, with an estimated thirty-six thousand left in the wild. Ranthambore National Park is where most of the natural history films about the biggest cats are recorded, as they have the largest population in the world. The park includes Ranthambore Ruins, an ancient fort dating back to the tenth century. Many iconic photographs show tigers basking in the sun on these ruins.

India is one of the largest countries in the world, so it was a two-day journey from Cochin to Rajasthan, including two flights and a four-hour bus ride. On the first night, we stayed at the Saj Ambagh

Palace. It is a five-star hotel that was once an actual palace of the rulers of the Indian state. It was all marble and opulence. The staff greeted us with rose petals, a flower lei, and a glass of champagne. My room felt like a queen's boudoir and had a balcony overlooking a formal garden populated by many peacocks. I felt like royalty.

After an early start with the peacocks as an alarm clock, we drove four hours to the Sujan-Sher Bagh Lodge, our accommodation in Ranthambore, for the next two days. On the long drive, I had time to observe the countryside. We were on a brand-new multi-lane highway that had just opened, but toll booths and rest areas were still under construction. This area was farm country in the dry season. Small plots of land were cultivated, but what fascinated me were the farms selling topsoil. I never heard of such a thing, but with the dry conditions and the wind, I understood why topsoil was a commodity. When we arrived in the town close to our accommodation, it was painfully obvious how poor these people were. The sacred cows were wandering freely, as is tradition, but they were scrounging around in the garbage for food as there was nothing green to see anywhere. We passed a woman making patties out of cow dung for cooking fuel. Pigs and half-naked children were running in the streets.

Sujan-Sher Bagh is outside the national park. When we arrived, the staff greeted us with ice-cold towels, champagne, and a safety briefing and escorted me to my gorgeous tent. I can get used to five-star living. What a contrast to what we witnessed outside the camp. When we arrived at my tent, I was greeted by the resident troop of langur monkeys playing on the roof. I couldn't wait to see the tigers.

Ranthambore was at the height of its dry season, and it was very hot, one hundred and seven degrees, but the mornings started off cool. Sweatshirts and provided knee blankets were called for in the mornings. By afternoon, we were sweating in our tee shirts and needed dark glasses for the glare, hats for shade as the jeeps had no roofs, and bandanas over our noses and mouths for the dust.

Ranthambore National Park Day One

The camp woke up at 5:15 am with bells, and ten minutes later, my pre-breakfast arrived at my door. I donned my bug spray, sunblock, and clothes, and I was all set to meet the Jeep driver and guide. There were four guests per jeep. Off we went to the park. Ranthambore is all about protecting the environment and tigers. The park is divided into ten areas, and guests' entry is limited to specific areas. As we went through park security, we were assigned our location for the day and had a different area each day. Only seven areas are open each day, and the park is closed during the three months of the monsoon season. This regulation reduces human encroachment on the cats with free range inside and outside the park. They can move around freely; we cannot. Since it was early morning, we hustled to the local watering hole as this was the perfect time to spot a cat. As luck would have it, a mother and her three feisty yearling cubs were getting a morning drink. How incredible.

Female tigers give birth about four times in their short life span, ten to fifteen years. This family included two sisters and one brother. As we watched the tigers soak and play in the water, it was evident that one of the sisters was the instigator of the bunch. As her brother soaked in the mud hole, she stalked him from behind and then pounced. He jumped up and snarled and batted her away. We watched all the shenanigans for a good forty-five minutes before Mom headed them away from the road, which was off-limits to us.

We moved away, searching for other wildlife. We saw two species of monkeys, two kinds of deer, lots of peacocks, and many species of birds, both endemic and migratory. At one point, we stopped to watch a group of peacocks, spotted deer, and monkeys, often seen together. Suddenly, the peacocks let out an alarm call, and all the animals started running. We then caught sight of a jackal chasing after a deer who luckily did not get caught. Peacock alarm calls are how the guides find tigers in the hot part of the day. Just follow the alarm calls, and you may spot a tiger.

Halfway through the game drive, we stopped at an overlook for "bush tea." The driver set out a white tablecloth on the jeep's hood with coffee, chai tea (the only kind I now drink), water, and cake. It was a lovely respite. A few hours later, we were back at the camp for breakfast. I wasn't hungry then, so I opted for some fruit. Lunch starts at noon, but the group agreed to meet about 1:30 pm before the 3 pm game drive.

On our second drive, we headed to an area near the ancient Ranthambore Fort. We stopped to look at the ancient ruins and were soon surrounded by hat and tee shirt hawkers. What caught my eye was the snake charmer squatting beside a rattan basket. He was totally unexpected. I was fascinated and went over to him. He took the lid off the basket and immediately started to play his pungi, a traditional wind instrument. As expected, but still fascinating, the large, hooded cobra slowly rose from the basket, seemingly entranced by the sound. After a few minutes, I tipped the charmer and returned to the jeep for our second drive of the day.

The area we were assigned was shaded and greener, but it was still one hundred and seven degrees; it felt like I was slowly roasting in an oven for three hours. I drank three bottles of water in four hours.

Again, we saw many birds, deer, and peacocks, but no more tigers. However, we did see an endangered sloth bear and her cub. There are only one hundred in this vast park, and they are primarily nocturnal, so for us to get to see them was very fortunate. We watched Mom dig at a termite mound for about forty minutes before we left them alone. Seeing this big, black, lumbering bear in the heat was remarkable. I thought I had it bad.

After a "sundowner" in the park of juices, gin & tonics, beer, soda, and cakes, we returned for a traditional Indian dinner with a tray holding about seven small bowls. Some were too spicy for me, but I could eat some, and they were delicious. Indian food was a first for me.

Ranthambore National Park Day Two

Up at 4:30 am for an early 5:30 am drive! Last one, unfortunately. We have now seen the big two (tigers and bears), so our goal on our last day was to spot a leopard. One of the jeeps in our group saw one on the first day, so we all had our fingers crossed. The area we were assigned is the farthest from our camp, so we had quite a drive to arrive there at sunrise. Area six was arid, with many trees and soaring cliffs above the dirt track. The day turned out to be all about birds, no leopards, but I did spot another jackal. It was one hundred and eight degrees. We spent the afternoon on a three-hour bus ride back to Jaipur Airport, a flight to Mumbai, and then a bus to meet the Luna at 11 pm. My second overland was just as exhausting as the first and just as wonderful.

Taj Mahal Agra

Harry had returned from his Taj Mahal overland an hour before me, and we immediately shared our experiences. He thoroughly enjoyed his tour of this incredible monument, which was all about love. They stayed overnight at a hotel close to the site, avoiding the crowds by going before sunset, staying for the moonrise, and returning at sunrise. The white native marble reflects the light, so the stone has an ethereal glow and can be gold, lavender, or pure white.

His guide was also a camera nerd. He took a picture of Harry sitting in the iconic Jackie Kennedy and Michelle Obama pose, seated on the bench, with the entire Taj Mahal highlighted behind them. The guide somehow manipulated that picture to create a reverse image so that Harry and his twin brother sat side by side. Harry has no brother. He treasures this picture as he should; we both do.

CHAPTER 24

The Other Half – Misconceptions

D URING my first attempt at a world cruise in 2022, I thought that Harry and I would be out of our depth. Before the 2022 and 2024 cruises, we signed up for a messaging group to get tips about what to bring, cabin storage, and private excursions. While reading posts by fellow passengers, I noticed they were older and had more money than we did. When my friends asked me about them, I always said, "They had more money than God." I know this is rude, but I was jealous.

In 2022, we did not socialize due to Covid19, so I did not know if my preconceived notion was valid. In 2024, I got to spend time with many fellow passengers and make some lifelong friends, and happily, I can say that I was all wrong. Yes, some passengers had been doing the world cruise many years in a row, and I did not have the means to do that. But there were many more who were hard-working dreamers like Harry and me.

I did, however, get to see how the other half lived. Harry and I were in a one-hundred-and-sixty-square-foot cabin with a couch and coffee table, a desk, our twin beds, and no window. My friend and fellow poker player, James, was in the top-of-the-line owner's suite, which was one thousand square feet. James was kind enough to invite us for drinks in his suite and for dinner in the Prime Grille. Harry and I were excited to see this space. These suites are at the ship's stern, so the balcony has a private view and is about three times bigger than a standard ship's balcony. When we knocked on James' door, we were greeted by the suite's butler and ushered into the main living, dining, and bar area. Of course, the butler had everything ready to offer us whatever drinks we wanted, and there were nuts, cheeses, and crackers on the coffee table.

James welcomed us in; Harry and I took seats on the large couch, and James sat in an overstuffed chair perpendicular to us. It seemed huge compared to our tiny space. The dining area had a table that sat six. And the bar was fully stocked. During one of the poker games, James asked me what Harry and I drank so he could have my favorite Bombay Sapphire Gin and Harry's Crown Royal waiting. James and I discussed the merits of some of the gin brands with aromatics added, and he suggested I try The Botanist brand of gin made in Scotland. Well, thank you, James. The butler seemed happy to replace my Sapphire with The Botanist and one sip of this smooth, dry G&T with extra lime, and I was hooked. So good!

James was gracious enough to offer a grand tour of the entire suite, and Harry and I couldn't wait to see the bathroom. The walk-in shower was three times the size of ours and could easily hold three people—not that we would try that. The bedroom had a full king-sized bed instead of the usual two twins pushed together.

Harry and I were both impressed and jealous of all that space. It was kind of James to share his private space with us, and I need to stop misjudging or judging people, it's a bad habit.

CHAPTER 25

Dubai – Bigger the Better

D UBAI'S government philosophy is to run the country like a business. It is clean and safe, and the cost of living is high. The Prime Minister of the United Arab Emirates (UAE) has built this city from reclaimed ocean and has absolute control over city planning. He is all about the biggest, the newest, and the most creative. Every high rise, and there are hundreds, is each different and architecturally spectacular. Dubai has the two tallest buildings in the world, and I am sure he plans to build even taller ones. I believe he has an issue with size.

I have always wanted to go to Dubai since I saw a picture of the hotel resembling a sailboat. The setting is also breathtaking; the hotel sits on a reclaimed beach surrounded by the ocean, with a bridge to access it. The Burg Al Arab Hotel has a seven-star rating (the only one globally) and consists of only suites. The price per night starts at sixteen hundred and seventy dollars, a reminder that this emirate is all about capitalism. Twelve percent of the population are Emiratis (native citizens), all millionaires. The other eighty-seven percent of the population are ex-patriots from two hundred and thirty countries. They are either workers brought in for high-paying jobs or the uber-rich.

SeaSpirit offered excursions to both iconic towers in Dubai: The Burg Khalifa, named after the Prime Minister's deceased brother and the tallest building in the world, and the Burg Al Arab. I could not wait to have tea in the Burg Al Arab.

We entered the hotel entrance, and the lobby soared to the top of the tower. The suite entrances circle the atrium on balconies. In the center, there is the most enormous Chihuly glass chandelier I have ever seen, and I have seen quite a few, as I am a big fan. The lobby area was richly decorated with several sitting areas with comfortable sofas and chairs, as well as a discreet check-in area.

We were met by a hotel employee and taken to a circular room on the fifty-sixth floor (top). The room had a spectacular two-hundred-degree view of the white sandy beaches and ocean below, with many chaise lounges and umbrellas. The room had round white tablecloth-draped tables with gilded porcelain place settings and champagne glasses.

We were served several varieties of teas, finger sandwiches, and dainty desserts. It was all elegant with white glove service. Before dessert, a server poured us each a glass of French sparkling apple juice with twenty-three-carat gold flakes floating throughout the bottle. It was delicious, and I wanted to see if I could purchase a bottle when I returned home, but I was sad to say that I would not be buying any at seventy dollars a bottle.

As we were leaving the hotel for our next stop on the excursion, I stopped in the ladies' room and was surprised by the most beautiful teal and sea-blue inlaid stall door. The expense of making these doors was significant. I now understood why this was a seven-star hotel.

Our next stop was to the souk (an open-air market). Since the Burg Al Arab was a bucket list item, I wanted to memorialize the visit with a tee shirt. I found a shirt with the hotel image on the front, and I wanted it to be dark purple with the white image. As I walked down the center of the market with vendors down each side, all wanting my attention, I picked one that seemed needy. I gave him my request and he had me wait in his "store" while he went off to find me what I wanted, and he did return with it. Since this is a bartering market, he gave me a price in UAE dirham, and I converted it to U.S. dollars. I knew the exchange rate and told the vendor I thought it was too much. He asked what I wanted to pay. Tee shirts in most ports were about ten dollars, so I did the math and put a number out there. That was my first mistake. Where was my trusty travel partner and financial advisor, Harry, when I needed him? I am now the proud owner of a lovely purple tee shirt with an image of the Burg Al Arab that cost me ninety-eight dollars!

We spent the night in Dubai, where SeaSpirit hosted our third special event for world cruisers. We were off to a desert party, and wow, what a party it was. Harry elected not to attend, so I went with some friends for the forty-five-minute drive into the desert.

The Sahara Encampment is a venue for tourists to be immersed in Bedouin life. The venue was quite large and thank goodness the rumor around the ship of us sitting on the ground was incorrect; we had comfortable chairs. They had three full buffets set up around the main stage. They also had a few activities scattered around. I participated in most. I had my hand henna 'ed and got my picture taken with a camel and a falcon. I decided to pass on the camel ride. The food was Middle Eastern and acceptably mild for us Westerners. But the show and the outdoor desert setting were the stars here.

The party's host was a local celebrity who was extremely overdressed in a sequined skintight ball gown and high heels. The entertainment included traditional drummers and North African whirling dervishes. The four men were closely spaced on the small stage and wore colorful wide skirts that ballooned as they spun. The costumes were electrified and lit up the night. They spun in place hundreds of times, getting increasingly faster, and then, at the exact moment, would switch positions and start all over again. I will never know how they did not get dizzy and vomit over the side of the stage.

There was also a belly dancer (think hula with a ridiculous hair-flipping routine). And finally, the most spectacular were the fire eaters and jugglers. By this time, it was pitch-black, with the only light coming from a myriad of stars above and fire. After ten minutes of watching their routine, we saw fireworks like the Fourth of July to the right of the stage. This went on for a while, and then the fire jugglers returned. We found out later that the fireworks were a bonus. The campsite next to our venue had fireworks. They were not part of our show. Overall, I loved being out in the desert and all that came with it.

When we left Dubai on our way to Africa, three hundred and eighty-five passengers remained out of the original six hundred and forty. The ship was less than half full, and there were four hundred crew members caring for us all. Harry and I could not have been more pleased as we could now have individual cabins. Don't get me wrong, Harry is my best friend, and I love him dearly, but privacy and not having to deal with mismatched sleep schedules was a beautiful thing for both of us.

As we sailed from Dubai, I envisioned the ship and everyone on it taking a deep breath. The tension from the itinerary change nightmare was over, and most passengers seemed to accept that, as we left for Africa.

CHAPTER 26

On Being Selfish

TWO dramatic incidents occurred halfway into the cruise that highlighted the two sides of selfishness. The first happened in a museum in Khasab, Oman. A young woman, who I did not recognize as a Luna passenger, and I were in the gift shop; I was looking at spices, and she was in the children's toy section. She yelled, "Can I get some help here?" with a distinctive American southern drawl. The sales counter was busy, and I saw no one available to help her. After a minute or two, she increased the volume of her voice and repeated her request. At that point, one of the salespeople came over to assist.

I went back to search for cinnamon. I then heard a commotion, and the young woman was verbally abusing this salesperson because they only had the floor model of the item she wanted to purchase. The poor salesperson did not deserve this tirade. The young woman then stomped out of the store, swearing. She is the poster child for the "ugly American."

In all my years of travel, I always go with the knowledge that I am a guest in whatever country I am visiting, whether bartering in a market or being given the privilege to enter someone's home. I therefore aspire to treat everyone I meet with respect, including their traditions, dress, and beliefs. There is no place for the "all about me" mentality.

The converse to the above occurred on the pool deck one sea day. As usual, I was out reading, and Gladys sat down beside me. I got to know her from my trivia team, and she was upset. She told me her longtime friends, Joshua and Annie, were struggling to live in their small cabin. At home, they live in a large house and have time away from each other. On the ship, they were constantly bickering. Gladys said she felt terrible because she did not want to spend more time with them.

I am always amazed that acquaintances and strangers think my advice is trustworthy. I beg to differ and have no idea why they think this of me, but I try my best to offer appropriate comments. In this instance and several other conflicts on this trip, my advice was to be selfish. A world cruise is a once-in-a-lifetime experience (for me, anyway), and it should be whatever you want it to be. Do not let anyone or anything ruin your ideal experience if you have the control to make it so. Be selfish.

CHAPTER 27

Seychelle Islands and East Africa – Tortoises, a Cyclone and Snares

WE crossed the equator for the third time on this journey. It seemed that the ship was ping-ponging back and forth between islands and not making any headway, but moving forward would mean our journey would end, and I did not want that to happen so soon.

Mahe, Seychelles

The Seychelles are an archipelago of islands in the Indian Ocean. There is a lot of beauty here but not much else. There is a corrupt government and a bad heroin problem. The island is lush, and there is fresh water and a plentiful food source, which was a draw to pirates.

Harry and I chose to go to the botanical garden to see one of Seychelle's claims to fame, the largest fruit in the world from the Coco De Mer palm tree. The trees are related to coconut palms, and the fruit shape suggests female and male human anatomy. I did say these are the most enormous fruits in the world. The government regulates how many female fruits go to market. They are highly prized and valuable. Unfortunately, the botanical garden had one stolen the week before we arrived. It is so regulated that the garden guides have never tasted them. The tree can grow outside of the Seychelles but will never bear fruit since their specific insect pollinator only lives on the island.

The garden also houses about a dozen giant Aldabra tortoises, a good food source for pirates. They have a life span of fifty years or more, and the garden has one hatched in 1832. They were celebrating his one hundred and ninety-first birthday! He is thought to be the oldest living land animal. Harry and I got to feed these incredible reptiles. Harry had no issues getting his tortoise to eat the fern he offered. Mine seemed to be a picky eater as he was not interested in the top of the fern but more interested in the thicker bottom portion and almost bit my finger off. They have substantial jaws.

As we were leaving, we bumped into our friend Steve, who was excited to share with me his Zen experience with his tortoise. He said there was an instant connection as soon as he saw the tortoise, so he sat down facing the animal, and they had a staring contest. He said they gazed deep into each other's eyes for at least ten minutes before the tortoise broke eye contact. He said it was amazing and something he will always cherish. I was jealous.

Steve is a nature lover like me. At one point, we talked about bird species, and I said I had two applications on my phone. One is to identify plants, and the second is to identify birds. So, he began sending me pictures of unknown birds to identify. No matter where I have traveled, birds have always fascinated me. Even after my first trip to Africa, when someone asked me which animal I liked best, it was the birds such as the regal secretary bird or the African eagle, not the giraffe or elephant.

When I was in Costa Rica many years ago, I met a woman who

was traveling alone as I was. Her husband was a high-end lawyer, and his trial date had changed, so he could not travel. She was the Chief Financial Officer at one of the most prestigious newspapers in the world. She was an avid birder, and she and I bonded. While everyone else in the group looked outward, she and I looked upward. Our guide was also into birds and told us that the record number of birds spotted on his tour was one hundred and forty-one in a week. He challenged us to break the record; he was the judge and kept track of the sightings. We did not break the record, but we almost did. We spotted one hundred and thirty-two species of birds. I wanted to track the species I would see on this trip and the application would help me do that. All told, I saw eighty-six species.

Tropical Cyclone Ialy

At dinner two days before arriving at Mombasa, Kenya, we got a warning from the Cruise Director that, based on the weather report, we expected to be in rough seas for the next twenty-four hours. I had my Meclizine tablets at the ready and, directly after dinner, I took a pill. I could feel the swells already. Unbeknownst to me, but not to the savvy internet surfers onboard, we were about to meet Tropical Cyclone Ialy and make the national news for the first time. The storm, which intensified from a tropical storm to a cyclone, brought wind gusts of more than forty-five miles per hour with twenty-foot seas.

That night, I slept well due to the drug, and the following day, I took another seasick pill as the storm was still raging outside. Thank goodness for the outside bow camera. It was my eyes to the outside world when I was in my cabin and a weather indicator every morning on what to expect. Several times in the morning, I felt better and tried to shower, but I kept bumping into the furniture in the cabin, so I sat back down and read some more. By mid-afternoon, the seas had calmed appreciably, and I showered and ventured out for a soothing meal of baguette slices with butter. The Luna's bakery chef makes the best baguettes.

I was returning to my cabin after my snack when I spotted Suzette, the ship's general manager, whose job is to keep the Luna in perfect shape, manage the crew, maintain overall safety, and crew training, and the list goes on. Suzette was in a hallway outside the elevators using a flashlight in a corner. With my curiosity piqued, I had to ask what she was doing. She told me she was hunting for dirt and dust. I can never invite her to my home. Suzette is from France and has a lovely French accent; once I picked up on that, I finished our conversation in French, my second language. We enjoyed chatting for a few minutes, and I wished her good dust hunting.

Mombasa, Kenya

I woke at 5 am today, and we had docked already in Mombasa, Kenya. This area of the world is famous for its rich and diverse wildlife and is a signature destination for those seeking a safari. Unfortunately, today, Kenya is also known for its poverty, political instability, ethnic tensions, and environmental issues such as deforestation and poaching.

After a quick breakfast, I left the Luna and expected to board a bus, but to my surprise, a long line of Toyota Land Cruisers was waiting at the gangway. I was disappointed to see these vehicles as they were not open to the air, and taking photographs would be difficult. Then I realized that the top went up, giving a three-hundred-and-sixty-degree open-air view.

The Cruisers held five passengers plus the driver. I saw two friends, and we headed off to the jeep with a couple already ensconced in the second-row seats. I would have preferred a bus to get us to Tsavo National Park, as the inside of the Land Cruiser was well-worn. As we made our way along a rutted, congested road full of big rig trucks, I noticed Bob's chair rocking backward at every bump. Since I was not six foot three, I offered to switch seats with him. That worked out better, as I could not feel the seat rocking when I was in it.

The two-hour ride to Tsavo National Park was an adventure that took three hours. The trucks hauling containers dominated the road, leaving the busy port of Mombasa. Traffic was at a snail's pace; it seemed like I was on a Los Angeles freeway in rush hour, except this road had two lanes. Mario Andretti must have trained the lead Land Cruiser driver. He led the rest of us over to the breakdown lane, and when that slowed down, he drove us through a small opening on a raised dirt road under construction that was not ready for public use. All the other drivers followed him. I was holding on for dear life as the road was bumpy. After a short time, I saw cement barriers up ahead and saw no way to get back to the actual road except to turn around. But somehow, he fit the vehicle through the narrowest of spaces and we continued on the unfinished road. After about five miles of this craziness, we did come to the end of the road. We could go no further; again, it seemed like we would need to turn around. Again, the lead driver found a small space with a three-foot severe drop to the main road, and he plunged headlong down this path. As I watched him, I held my breath as he nosed-dived down the incline into the same heavy traffic we had left behind. It was our turn next, and our driver was just as fearless. I can't say how much time we saved having this off-road adventure, but I was sure the safari would be less dramatic.

Once we entered Tsavo National Park, the Land Cruisers put up their roofs so we could stand up and take pictures. The park has many different areas, and we took off to our assigned area. This park has no rhino, so if we were lucky, we would see four of the "big five": lion, leopard, elephant, and cape buffalo. Also, the area we were assigned had no tall trees, so even though they lived in the park, we saw no giraffes. Our first sighting was of the famous Tsavo "red" elephants. These animals are so named because the soil in Tsavo is a vibrant red clay, and elephants love to take mud baths to coat their sensitive skin. It makes them stand out and easier to see. As it was the heat of the day, we saw no cats and only a few buffalos.

As we headed out of the park, the driver stopped the car, took his rifle, and walked off the trail about thirty yards. On a small bush was a devastating sight. An impala was hanging with its neck in a noose and struggling. We were lucky the driver had great eyes, could untangle the antelope, and set her free. Impalas are the daintiest and prettiest of the antelopes. They have striking facial markings and long eyelashes, making them appear as though they were wearing makeup.

As we exited the park, the driver reported the incident to the authorities, but nothing was expected to change. The bush meat trade is prevalent in Kenya. The people here live in poverty and this is a free way to get meat to feed their families. The parks do not have enough rangers to patrol the thousands of acres nor the money to pay additional staff. It is a losing proposition.

I was thankful we could save one small life but saddened by the poaching situation. My first time at this park was in 1980, and there were thirty-five thousand elephants; today, there are only sixteen thousand remaining.

Zanzibar, Tanzania

Zanzibar is a small autonomous archipelago and, like most of East Africa, is poor. In the first three minutes of leaving the ship, it was obvious that this country had no governmental services, as there was garbage everywhere.

I elected to go to the Jonzani Forest to see blue monkeys and the endangered, endemic red Columbus monkeys. This is the only place in the world where they live; their population is estimated to be fifty-eight hundred. My world was rocking when I got to the forest and disembarked the bus. It was muddy with standing water since it had rained. When I started to walk toward the trail I was rocking. It is not unusual for me to get off the ship and feel like I am still on it. But most times, I am not about to start a trek into a muddy forest, so I decided to return to the bus.

Before you feel sorry for me, I saw many blue monkeys eating breakfast in the trees right next to the bus. Ten minutes later, it started to pour, and my fellow passengers high-tailed it back and joined me. I saw more monkeys than they did. Our next stop was to see the red Columbus monkeys in a different forest area. On the road, we saw one sheltering from the rain in a tree with large leaves, which was acting like an umbrella. Clearly, she was not enjoying the downpour as she was making herself as small as possible, huddled under a leaf. Their fur is a mix of red and brown, but their backs are all red, hence their name. They weigh about twenty pounds and usually live in a large group, although this one was going solo. They have four fingers on their hands and five on their feet, which allows them to use all four appendages as hands. I would find that helpful.

The East Africa that I saw in 2024 was not what I remembered from 1980, which could be due to my lousy memory or political upheaval and economic pressures. The abject poverty here made me aware of my privileged life and how thankful I was that I was born in America.

CHAPTER 28

The Seals

THE day following our departure from Zanzibar, I was going about my regular sea day routine. I was having breakfast with Harry in the buffet, and I noticed two passengers that I had never seen before. They stood out as being different. Both were young, in their thirties was my guess, and both were highly buff, muscles everywhere. They were also easy to look at. We knew a new tech team was coming aboard to upgrade the wiring for a much-needed wi-fi boost, but they seemed to have too many muscles for that. As usual, I verbalized my imagined thoughts to Harry about who they were and what they were doing on board. None of my suppositions came close to their actual purpose.

After breakfast, Harry went to the walking track to get in his miles, and I went to the main pool deck to get some sun and read. One of the gentlemen was on the track doing lunges and sprints, which was lovely to watch. I saw Gayle and Steve on the other side of the pool deck, gawking between shots of their daily ping pong match. Harry, totally out of character, synced up with the gentleman and started chatting. I knew Harry would get the real story at that point, so I returned to reading.

During the poker tournament that afternoon, I sat next to Dexter, who told me he had met an ex-Navy Seal named Gabe in the gym and got all the details. Gabe was thirty-seven and did one tour in Iraq and one in Afghanistan. He and his partner Tony, who was forty-one, were on board to protect the passengers and the ship from pirates. Well, my jaw dropped! I had heard about pirates off the coast of Somalia because I had seen the movie "Captain Phillips". I did not think it applied to cruise ships, and we were past the Somali coast. It turns out that the coast of West Africa is now a hotbed of pirating, with twenty-one attacks in 2023; who knew? Gabe also told Dexter that Tony was with him in

Afghanistan and they both made five hundred dollars a day without benefits for their consulting work. They were scheduled to disembark in the Canary Islands. I was impressed with Dexter's sleuthing ability and gave him kudos. He went on to win the tournament; I came in second.

Harry and I went to One Eighty before dinner to meet the gang and have a cocktail. I knew Harry had something on his mind, but I figured he would tell me when he was ready. He had waited to tell us all at the same time. He stated that Tony was forthcoming and friendly. He informed Harry that all the passengers were to receive the dreaded SeaSpirit mail when we returned to our cabins after dinner, which would explain pirating countermeasures and tactics for the upcoming days. He mentioned two drills planned for the next two days.

After dinner, we went directly to our cabin to retrieve the mail. The letter stated that we were on pirate protocols starting immediately, which meant nightly blackouts. This involved shutting off most of the outside lights except for the bare minimum needed to provide enough light to move around without hurting ourselves. All outside-facing windows were to have the curtains closed from dusk to dawn, including on the balcony and suites. All balcony doors were to be locked at all times. Tomorrow, the first drill was about training the crew on safety procedures. That was manning the hallways with walkie-talkies, which is the same procedure done during lifeboat drills and then following any instructions they receive from the captain. The crew area managers were also assigned curtain checks, including all balconies. We were asked to stay out of the way of the drill.

However, the following day was the passenger drill, and we were all required to attend. After the captain's announcement, balcony and suite cabin passengers were to proceed to the hallway directly outside their cabins and have a seat until further directed. Balconies could be an entry point for pirates.

As Harry and I looked at each other, it became clear that we were not in Kansas anymore. This was serious. So much for no drama, but hopefully, the Seals would protect us. I did feel safer with them onboard and appreciated the cruise line for hiring them.

CHAPTER 29

Overland Kruger – The Big Five, Guns, and A Charge

I ALWAYS knew that if I got back to South Africa, I wanted to go to Kruger National Park, so when the itinerary changed, it was my number one priority to find a way to accomplish this. When the overland trip information arrived in the ship's mail, I was thrilled to see five Kruger options listed. They were about the same amount of time, but the difference was how long you spent in the park versus outside doing other things, including traveling. I chose one of the two options with the most time in the park. The difference between them was the camp. Since it was dry season, I wanted the option with cabins right on the river's edge. Since Harry had done so well choosing a lottery ticket, I got my first choice and was elated.

Kruger National Park is one of Africa's largest and oldest game reserves, spanning just under five million acres or about the size of Massachusetts. Established in 1898, it is renowned for its diverse wildlife, including the iconic Big Five: lion, elephant, Cape buffalo, leopard, and rhinos. The park is also home to a wide variety of other species, including cheetahs, giraffes, zebras, hippos, and crocodiles, all living in diverse ecosystems, including savannahs, woodlands, and rivers.

Jock Safari Lodge is the only lodge within Kruger National Park boundaries and is situated on the Motomeni River. We could go anywhere within the park boundaries, but non-guests were not allowed on the six thousand acres belonging to the lodge. When we arrived, we were greeted and introduced to the entire staff, and we checked in. We listened to the safety briefing about locking doors and never leaving the cabin without an escort after dark. They told us a leopard had been seen on the property the night before. Hopefully, we would be so lucky. We were escorted to our cabin, not a tent, (Harry was happy), but with solid walls and a thatched roof. The beds were draped in mosquito netting. We had already started taking our malaria medication and had plenty of bug spray.

The cabin was impressive and disappointing at the same time. We had our own little compound. As we walked through the gated entrance to our cabin, there was a small private cold pool, an outdoor shower, a bathtub, and several chaises, all on a wooden deck overlooking the river. There was a screened tent at the edge of the riverbank with a double day bed facing the river. There was only one thing missing: water. I knew it was the dry season. I did not realize that this river is seasonal, and during the dry season, there is no water to be found anywhere! It was, however, peaceful and serene. I did spend many of my free hours during the heat of the day, outside under the tent, watching and listening to the insects and birds and contemplating my wonderful life. Harry spent the time inside napping.

First Game Drive

Late in the afternoon, we met our driver/guide, Jabari, as he placed the loaded rifle on the dashboard. We then left for our first of four game drives. Our road for game drives was the riverbed, which was about twenty-five feet across and, in some places, eight feet deep. It was mostly sand with a smattering of short, dry grass. It did not take long for us to spot wildlife as they also use the riverbed as a road. In three hours, we saw the big five (lion, leopard, buffalo, elephant, and rhino). This is unheard of to see all five in such a short time. Even Jabari was shocked. On the way back to the lodge, we stopped for sundowners, drinks, and a snack, as we watch the sun go down over the dry riverbed.

The first night, we were instructed to be ready at 7:30 pm to be escorted down to the riverbed for a barbecue dinner. As we walked down, I pointed out to Harry that the electric fences around the camp did not extend to the riverbed. We were on the outside, looking in. And the delicious aromas coming from the barbecue pit were mouthwatering. I can only imagine where all the lions, leopards, and hyenas were headed. As we took our seats at the only available table, my level of anxiety rose a notch. The area was lit by torches strategically placed by the buffet table and scattered among the seating areas. A fire pit behind us provided light for the armed guards sitting around it and for the table where Harry and I sat. The presence of the guards made me feel safe and scared, as the last thing I wanted to experience was those rifles being used.

I heard hyenas calling in the distance as we returned to our seats after getting barbecued impala and warthog. I hoped they would stay far away. They eat anything and can smell food within a five-mile radius. Our meal was scrumptious, and as we waited for dessert, I heard the distinctive high-pitched whoops and "laughter" from a hyena that seemed to be coming from right behind the fire pit, where it was pitch-black. I was not the only one hearing this as all three guards rose as one and spread out to the edge of the light. The eerie laughter came again nearer than before, followed by a rifle shot in the air as a warning. The camp manager appeared and told us, "You should not worry. We never had a problem at the weekly barbeque." I decided against dessert, and Harry and I headed back to our cabin with an escort.

As I crawled into bed, I noticed a palm-sized Baboon Spider crawling inside my mosquito netting. My worst nightmare. As far as wildlife goes, spiders are my only phobia. I immediately jumped out of bed, pointed this creature out to Harry, and said, "Do something!" He grabbed the greeting letter from the lodge's general manager, slid into the netting, and gently coaxed the spider onto the letter. I was in the corner cowering. Harry then slipped out from under the netting, went out the door, and calmly released the spider. Harry is my hero. I then searched the entire cabin but found no more spiders. I was exhausted after a remarkable and event-filled day. I climbed back under the mosquito netting, and the next thing I knew, I heard the telephone ringing.

Second Game Drive

The 5 am wake-up call came about three hours too early for me. But I was excited to get back to the wilderness. It was a fifty-degree morning, so layers and a lap blanket were needed. We headed down to the riverbed and quickly spotted a small herd of elephants browsing. The elephants were wandering in our direction. Jabari informed us that it appeared to be all females with a juvenile male. As they continued forward, we soon were in the middle of them. Jabari thought slowly backing up the jeep and leaving these animals in peace was the way to go. As he backed up, I glanced behind us and oops, there was a male about fifteen yards away. Harry grabbed my leg and gave me his "I do not like this" look. I gave him a thumbs up, as speaking at this moment was inadvisable. We were surrounded! The male showed the telltale signs of concern for his family by flapping his ears, stamping a foot, and vocalizing his displeasure. The females did not seem to be bothered by us, but the young male took his job of protecting his family seriously. Jabari put the jeep in drive, and we slowly inched forward to give the male as much space as possible, and the female in front of us slowly moved off. Another close call and an adrenaline-pumping encounter.

We moved further down the riverbed and saw a Greater Kudu, a large, majestic brown-red antelope with striking white markings and long, thin, spiral horns. We also spotted a mother white rhinoceros and her yearling calf. The mom and baby were browsing on the edges of the embankment, and the mom seemed unaffected by our presence. The baby, however, seemed curious. The driver stopped the jeep in the middle of the river, and we sat and watched them. The youngster approached the front of the jeep, he took three steps toward us and the looked back at Mom to see if this got any reaction from her as if to say, "Look at me; I am brave." He got five yards from us, stopped, and stared at this big object before him. He was no longer curious but wanted to show us who was boss. The yearling weighed about one thousand pounds, our jeep weighed about five thousand pounds, and mom weighed about five thousand pounds. Hopefully, she was not compelled to come and protect her baby.

The baby rubbed its feet in the sand, seemingly trying to get some traction for a headlong assault and ran straight at us. I was in awe, scared, and holding my breath as he charged. A direct hit to the engine could cause problems, and more importantly, I was concerned about the baby. Jabari said nothing; none of us did. One foot from the unmoving jeep, the rhino stopped dead in its tracks. He decided we were too big to tackle. He shook himself off and sauntered back to Mom's side. I finally took a breath. Another adrenaline rush.

I was ready for a meal and a rest before we headed out for the afternoon drive. I love to try new foods, and they had guinea fowl, a grouse-like bird, on the lunch menu. I am glad I tried it, but I will not order it again soon.

Third Game Drive

When we headed for the afternoon drive, Jabari asked us if we wanted to see anything specific. I was surprised when Harry spoke up and requested a male lion. We saw a mom and her cubs yesterday, but there were no males. I did not think it could get any better as we had already seen so much. Kruger did not disappoint us as the driver had a spot in mind to find a territorial male lion. We left the riverbed and Jock property and headed deeper into the park.

The park's roads are paved, and visitors are required to stay on them. There is no off-roading here. As we passed other jeeps or trucks, Jabari stopped and chatted in Swahili with the other drivers. This is the park's communication network. They shared animal sightings and any news of the day. One driver shared a wild dog sighting with us, so we immediately turned around and headed in that direction.

Wild dogs are very rare. There are only sixty-six hundred animals worldwide. I was lucky enough to see them twice when I was in the Okavango Delta in Botswana. The Kenyan population is highly endangered, with less than three hundred, and they are being wiped out by monkeypox. The painted dogs, as they are known because of their spotted coats, live and hunt in packs of an alpha male and female with their offspring. They compete for food with lions and hyenas and are not the top predator here.

Kruger's two hundred-and-eighty animals are also highly endangered but they have not been infected with monkeypox. I had my fingers crossed, hoping we would be lucky enough to find them. We were even more fortunate. As we got closer to the area where they were spotted, Jabari slowed down, and as we went around a curve, we saw two dogs standing on the road directly in front of us. As we got near, we saw a truck pulled over and assumed they were watching. It turns out they were researchers who were in the middle of putting a radio collar on a dog. What luck! They had already tranquilized a wild dog and were waiting for it to take effect. The other two dogs were waiting on their alpha, and they seemed uneasy: sitting, getting up and pacing, and sitting again.

When the tranquilizer had the desired effect, one of the two researchers went into the high grass, gently lifted the dog, and placed him on the truck's lift gate. We watched as one took blood samples and measurements and the second fitted the dog for its collar. They then tested the radio signals and gently returned the dog to the same spot where they had first picked him up. They gave him an antidote to the anesthetic, and within a few seconds, the dog took off with his pack mates close behind. The researchers then told us they were using the Kruger population to discover a way to protect all wild dogs against monkeypox. I wish I were fifty years younger so I could do this kind of research.

By this time, the sun was setting, so it was time to face the west and toast the day. I chose gin and tonic, and Harry had a can (yes, a can) of white wine, both of which hit the spot. It was dark when we left the lookout and slowly headed back to the lodge. Before we left, Jabari pulled out the big spotlight connected to the battery.

I do not know how Jabari managed to drive and steer the jeep, sweeping the spotlight from side to side on both sides of the road as we searched for eye shine. The eyes of nocturnal animals all reflect light, causing their eyes to glow yellow or orange when hit with a spotlight. That is what he and all of us were searching for. We spotted birds and antelopes on the road as they feel safe because they can see in all directions.

After a few miles, off the road, in the high grass sat a majestic male lion. This was a perfect spot for him to ambush an unsuspecting gazelle for dinner. Harry got his wish and smiled from ear to ear as we sat and contemplated this king of all beasts.

When we arrived back at the lodge for a quick shower and dinner, we were greeted by the camp manager and his assistant. They offered us a welcome drink that was local to the area. Harry and I both had to try it. It is made from the Amarula fruit of the Elephant Tree, so named because the elephants love the fruit. The fruit starts to ferment when it ripens and falls on the ground. That is when the elephants search for it, and it gets them tipsy. I cannot quite picture a drunk elephant, but it happens. Amarula Cream Liquor is made from this sweet, sour, and citrusy fruit. It was delicious. Harry and I immediately went into the gift shop and bought a bottle to take home. However, mine never made it home, as I shared it with my trivia team and poker buddies. It was a hit all around.

It was another full day, and I was exhausted. In the middle of the night, I heard Harry whispering in a panicked voice, "Are you awake." And then I heard it. There was a loud munching sound by the side of the cabin. We both crept out of bed and followed the sound to the bathroom window. I slowly opened the frosted window to look out.

Standing right before us, not two feet away, was a big male elephant with a mouthful of green leaves. I smiled at Harry and slowly closed the window, leaving the elephant alone to enjoy his dinner. Harry was still concerned, but I calmed him down by explaining that we were no threat to the elephant and that he was no threat to us. We went back to bed, and it took me a while to fall back to sleep. The next thing I knew, the phone was ringing with our wake-up call.

Fourth Game Drive

It was another early morning and a cold start. As we headed out, I had no expectations of a spectacular day as we had already seen so much in such a short time. But it would make no difference if all I saw were antelopes or birds; being out in nature in this incredible environment was enough for me. We did not see much for the first hour of the drive, but the last hour was awesome.

Jabari spotted a lion on the ground under a tree, and we stopped to get a better look. But what was going on around the lion was mind-blowing. National Geographic would have loved to film the scene.

A large male leopard was in a very tall Umbrella Thorn tree and had dragged its late-night impala kill up the tree to protect it from lions and hyenas. A pride of lions, consisting of three lionesses and two males (probably brothers), were circling and eyeing the tree, trying to find a way up. There were also three hyenas on the outskirts contemplating their next meal. The two males climbed up a slanted lower branch, got about halfway up, and had no purchase to go any higher. They realized that their weight on the limb would cause the whole tree to shake, so the higher of the two started pouncing on the branch to shake the tree.

Meanwhile, the leopard grabbed the impala in its teeth and dragged it further into the canopy. When shaking had no effect, the lions tried climbing higher but could get no closer. They jumped to the ground and sent two females up to try. The lighter and more agile females made it higher into the tree than the males, but they were not quite close enough, so they both climbed down. They seemed to understand that this was futile.

Four of the five lions gave up and laid down under the tree. This looked like a stalemate. Who would leave first? The leopard had the upper hand here as he had dinner for at least two days. The lions would need to go hunting. The fifth lion kept circling the tree, seemingly plotting his next move. At one point, you could see his frustration as he took off after one of the hyenas but gave up and kept looking at the leopard. After a few minutes, he again jumped up to the branch and started shaking the tree with all his might. You could feel his frustration as the leopard looked down on him calmly. The lion jumped down again, growled his frustration, and moved off. His brother followed and growled back. The males then turned on each other, roaring and attacking each other; my guess was to release the pent-up frustration. They abruptly stopped after determining who was boss and wandered off, with the three females trailing behind.

Now that our time in Kruger was done, we returned to the lodge for a quick shower and lunch before heading to the airport. There was a park exit gate at a small airport, about an hour away from our lodge, giving us another hour in the park. Again, it did not disappoint. We stopped to watch and then followed a lioness who looked in some duress. She was continually chuffing and calling for her pride. It seemed she had lost them somehow. She looked sad and forlorn. The cries she was making were heart-wrenching to me.

We flew from Kruger to Cape Town and stayed at the five-star Taj Hotel while awaiting the Luna's arrival. The hotel boasted a view of the iconic Table Mountain, which was lovely at sunset. After a hot tub for me and a shower for Harry, we ordered room service and crashed. It was a busy and amazing few days, and I will never forget them.

CHAPTER 30

South Africa

I LANDED at Johannesburg airport a few years back for a transfer to Botswana, so I cannot say I have been there. I had always wanted to visit since it is considered the gateway to Kruger National Park, but I also knew about its appalling political history and its natural resources, diamonds, and vineyards.

Since Harry and I did not get back on the ship until 9 am and we had to leave for the SeaSpirit Luna special event at 11 am, we had no time for any other excursions. I could not have stomached visiting Robben Island Prison, where the late great Nelson Mandela was imprisoned for twenty-seven years for peacefully protesting the inequality and injustice of the black South African people, so it was just as well.

The special event was a meal and a show, as they all were, but this one was in the afternoon. All the world cruisers hopped on buses, and we drove about an hour outside of Cape Town to Kyalami to see the Lipizzan stallions. I had been to Vienna, Austria, where the first line of these gorgeous animals came from, and I was unaware of how they got to South Africa.

The roots of the South African Lipizzan trace to two individuals, both immigrants to South Africa who were each born in Eastern Europe: A horse breeder, Count Elemér Janković-Bésán de Pribér-Vuchin of Hungary, and a horse trainer, Major George Iwanowski of Poland. These two had to flee their homelands in 1944 due to the advance of the Red Army. After bringing their eight Lippizans, six mares, and two stallions, through Germany and England, they landed in South Africa in 1948, where they founded The South African Lipizzaner, a riding academy, a breeding center, and a training facility for these horses, which operates according to the classical model in which women ride and train their forty Lipizzan stallions.

Since seeing Vienna's training center and performances, I have researched and learned how these animals are trained to prance and jump in ways not typical of their natural behavior. The stallions are cruelly treated with heavy weights placed on hooves and whips to make them perform. The females are used solely to breed. I wish I could say the South African horses were treated differently, but the lead horsewomen who put all the five horses through their paces had a long whip which she did not hesitate to use. I did not stay to see the entire performance but walked outside to the corral to feed the horses some carrots.

When the performance was complete, they herded us into a large tent where a delicious lunch was served. After lunch, they had several activities to keep us occupied for two hours. They had women face painters in traditional bright-colored clothes and a live band. Many guests got up to dance, including Steve and Gayle, after a bit of coaxing from me. They had a diverse craft market, which I was excited about. We were each allowed to choose one item as a gift. If we selected any other items, we could negotiate pricing and purchase them. I bought a few mementos to take home as gifts and to display in my home.

CHAPTER 31

West Africa – Pelicans, Teeter Totters, and The Other Seals

WE were now in pirate waters! The Seals were busy every night doing curtain checks in all the common areas. The outside deck is void of light, with one exception. The pool bar has a turquoise light under the countertop, which was left on. I avoided walking through the pool deck at night and stayed indoors until we left the shores of West Africa. And if that was not enough to concern us, we were warned about an active Listeria outbreak, a nasty bacterial infection affecting several countries we planned to visit. We were warned not to eat or drink anything on shore.

Walvis Bay, Namibia

Walvis Bay is a haven for sea vessels because of its natural calm and sheltered deep-water harbor, but it is also a haven for wildlife. Since the once-endangered Southern Right Whales sought sanctuary here to give birth, it also attracted whalers in years gone by.

My excursion started five minutes from the Luna, from one pier to another, and I was off in a small motorboat to search for sea creatures. The boat had three seats up in the bow, and as I was one of the first passengers, I chose a seat up front, thinking I would have the best view. That was not the best choice. It was a foggy morning and in the low fifties, I had planned for multiple layers of clothes, and a blanket was provided, but it was still cold with the wind blowing in our faces.

We immediately started to see Cape Fur Seals in the water. After about fifteen minutes on the boat, a visitor hopped onboard – a fur seal. Five seals had been habituated to this boat with fish to entice them to stay for a short visit. I have mixed feelings about feeding wild animals; in most cases, it harms them. However, these seals displayed natural behavior, which did not seem to adversely affect them in this case. As the Seals disembarked, we headed to the main seal colony, and as I looked ahead, I spotted a large bird flying directly at me. Thank goodness the pelican had excellent navigational skills and landed not two feet in front of me on the boat's nose. He had cream-colored feathers and orange legs and feet. His bill was yellow with shades of blue and lavender. He was a handsome bird. He stayed for his fish breakfast, and we set off again for the primary seal colony.

On the way, we passed an area of oyster farms. The high concentration of nutrients in the cold water and intense sun makes it ideal for growing oysters. We had a chance to taste a sample, and it was delicious. As we approached the main Cape Fur Seal colony, we were escorted by thousands of seals playing in the water around us and making their typical barking vocalizations. As we got closer to the colony, the cacophony was deafening, and the ammonia smell was overpowering. We hugged the coastline, moving away from the colony, and encountered a tidal pool full of flamingos and Cape Cormorants.

We also saw two jackals hunting on the beach. And if that was not enough, we saw two species of dolphins, Heaviside and Atlantic Bottlenosed, on the way back to the Luna. It was another day I will never forget, seeing this vibrant bay teeming with life. Walvis Bay is a place I would love to come back to.

Sekondi-Takoradi, Ghana

Early in the morning, we crossed the equator for the fourth and final time. It was surreal that this six-month world cruise was almost at its conclusion. I was trying to focus on being in the moment and not thinking about my return home, but the days were flying by.

When Harry and I got on the bus for our city tour, we noticed a significant police presence. We were to have an escort all day. We should have felt safe with a police vehicle taking us around, but that makes you wonder why we needed one in the first place. After a forty-minute drive in a four-bus caravan with a police car in front, behind, and in the middle driving over dirt and poorly paved roads, we made our way to the shipbuilding area and the fishing port. On this drive, we saw nothing but abject poverty. The tiny stores along the side of the road were made of a few cinder blocks and a corrugated piece of tin as a roof. Most had a person seated in a plastic chair, selling whatever goods were their specialty. If they were selling buckets, they had three hanging up on display. Everything for sale was brightly colored as if they were trying to mask the meagerness of their offerings by drawing your attention to what they had. There was no abundance here. Yet Ghana is doing better than most West African countries. They have natural resources such as diamonds, coal, gold, cocoa, and shipbuilding. The average yearly income is two thousand dollars, it is relatively peaceful, and they accept migrants from many surrounding countries.

As we approached the port, we saw a small area on the shoreline crammed with boats in the process of being built. Two types of boats were built here: wooden trawlers big enough for a crew of ten to live in until their holds were full of fish and fifty-foot-long wooden pirogues with rows of benches.

As we parked the buses in a rutted, unpaved parking lot, we were asked to stay on the bus until the police indicated it was safe to exit. Each group of ten or so set off in a different direction with a police escort. This port was a hive of activity. There were about two dozen trawlers with laundry drying in the rigging and men moving about preparing to set sail in the late afternoon. The boats fish all night, return in the morning to sell their catch, and prepare to go out again that afternoon. All the boats take Tuesday off, so the fish have a day of rest.

At that time, in the morning, boats were in various stages of preparation. Some were checking and repairing nets, some were jockeying at the two fuel pumps, and some were packing the hold with ice needed to keep the catch fresh while out at sea. It was chaos, with boats moving from one dock area to another, jostling for position. Many times, these boats would run into each other or rub against each other. It was every man for himself.

Mindelo São, Vicente Island, Cape Verde Archipelago

Today, Harry and I went by large bus on a narrow Portuguese-built, one-hundred-year-old, inlaid, curvy, and steep stone road to the top of the dormant volcano on São Vicente. It was scary, with hairpin turns and large buses coming down the mountain at us. The view there should have been much better, but we were literally in the clouds.

We then made our way down the mountain to the beach. This is a volcanic island, so the beach should have black sand. There were black lava rocks here, but they were covered with tons of Saharan white sand that blows from mainland Africa. This is the same sand that makes it all the way to the United States as dust between July and August and causes the East Coast to be hazy.

When was the last time you were on a teeter totter? Harry spotted a playground across the street from the beach with a seesaw, so off we went. The last time I had been on a teeter totter was when I was about seven years old and broke my leg, but I am a big girl now, so I thought, "what the hey!" I had Harry do all the work; I was along for the ride. Halfway through, Harry took out his camera and started to video the experience. If I had not been laughing hysterically, I would have done the same to him. When was the last time you experienced unadulterated pure joy? It took me back to my six-year-old self, and to this day, when I think about the experience or re-watch the video, all I can do is grin.

The Gambia

When we docked in The Gambia, there were native dancers in traditional costumes made of cotton in bright vibrant colors and patterns waiting to dance for us. They also set up a vendor market on the dock. Judy had told us about a planned Toga Party that evening. She kept reminding us in the days leading up to this event that we were not allowed to use bed sheets but that the ports we visited had many places to buy inexpensive African material to put a toga together. The ship would provide all the safety pins. I love colorful prints but was not very interested in a toga party and did not think I would use the material for any other purpose. However, when I wandered the market, I spotted a material that spoke to me. It had a black background with white lattice work and bright cerulean daisies. The piece they were selling was six yards for twenty dollars. I was happy to add a few dollars to the economy, so I bought it and coerced Harry, who wanted nothing to do with a toga party or any other kind of costume party, to help drape and pin the material onto my body. I don't know how we accomplished it, but with only six safety pins and a paisley tee shirt, my costume was a hit and never fell off. It was great fun. I loved the print so much that I had a jacket made from it when I returned home.

The countries of West Africa are all poor, have few natural resources, and have high unemployment rates. There is nothing here. It was depressing to think about these people and their everyday lives, especially as I have so much for which I am grateful.

CHAPTER 32

The Rescue

LATE afternoon, while we were upstairs in One Eighty with friends having a drink and celebrating a birthday, Judy alerted us to an emergency call from a stranded boat two hours from our location. We were the closest boat. So, as maritime time law requires, we altered our course and went to assist. I first thought this could be a plot by pirates to be brought aboard the Luna. When I shared my thoughts with the group, we all agreed we were happy to have the Seals onboard and hoped they could deal with whatever was to come next.

Our group went up to Prime Grille to continue the birthday celebration. The seas were rough, and I felt queasy being on the top floor in the bow. I was feeling the swells. Many of the diners kept leaving their seats to look out the window, but it was dark, and there was not much to see but our reflections in the window. But after more than two hours, a guest stated that there was what appeared to be an oil tanker with its spotlight trained on a small pirogue. We watched as the Luna edged closer to the small boat. At that time, Judy announced that the evening show would be in the One Eighty Lounge and that the Stage Left Theater was off limits for the foreseeable future as it was where our new "guests" would be accommodated. She asked us to avoid being looky-loos and give these people some privacy.

The brave crew of the Luna, wearing impervious, protective jumpsuits, gloves, and masks, struggled to grapple hook the pirogue alongside our ship and secure it to the tender platform on deck three. Tony stood armed and ready on the tender platform. The six-foot waves threatened the crew's lives as they maneuvered all sixty-two people from the pirogue to the Luna and up the stairs to the crew "highway." This wide corridor runs from the bow to the stern and is the passageway for moving large pallets of food and supplies around the ship. It is also where the crew can move quickly from one area of the vessel to another to do their duties. One end of the corridor was designated a makeshift triage and intake area, with Gabe and a medical team standing by.

The crew first brought two women and one child onboard, and they were taken to an area screened in to provide privacy where a freshwater shower area had been installed. Suzette told them in French to strip and discard all their clothes into a hazardous materials bin. They were then hosed off and given towels and a protective jumpsuit. The crew took all able-bodied folks aboard one at a time, and they were told to sit in the designated area to wait their turn in the "shower." Several guests needed assistance getting aboard, and the crew carried these up to triage, where the doctor was waiting with stretchers and medical equipment. Five souls on the small boat had passed away from their ordeals, and three of them were taken aboard to the morgue. Due to the worsening weather conditions, two were left at sea, as it was too dangerous to try to maneuver them out of the pirogue and onto the ship. A GPS tracker was left in the boat, and the information was given to the coast guard in Tenerife so they could retrieve the bodies once the storm had passed.

After each guest had showered and changed, they were escorted to Stage Left, where all the coffee tables and chairs had been clustered around the outer edges of the large space, leaving the middle ready as a sleeping area. As each guest entered, they were given bedding and shown a place to sleep. They were given a water bottle and directed to the filtered water system in the theater, where they could refill their bottles as needed. On the back bar, sandwiches and hot soup were also available. The women and child were isolated on the stage. When every guest was accounted for, the doctor checked on each person. They also had two restrooms at each entrance to Stage Left. This was their temporary home while they were with us, and they had to stay in this isolated area.

These people were either refugees fleeing the abject poverty in Senegal to search for a better life or pirates. This journey by pirogue is a three or four-day trip to Tenerife in the Canary Islands. They had been at sea for twenty days. They were all severely dehydrated and starving, except two of the oldest men, who seemed healthier than the rest. Most of these people were in their late teens or twenties, but it was hard to tell in their emaciated state. One of the younger men was in deplorable condition and required I.V. therapy with a sugar infusion. Unfortunately, he did not make it through the night.

As the guests settled in, several crew members removed bundles of belongings from the pirogue. With the watchful eye of John, the First Mate, the crew searched the belongings. All the clothes and perishables were discarded. Passports and personal mementos were cleaned and placed in a bag to return to its rightful owner. Two of the bundles contained nasty-looking knives and were confiscated. The secondary door to Stage Left was locked and secured, and the main door was closed. One of the Seals was stationed at this door until the guests disembarked. No one had yet ruled out pirates.

CHAPTER 33

First Day After the Rescue – Questions

AT the daily 9 am Cruise Director's announcement, Judy told us that we had sixty-two new guests aboard and that the Stage Left Theater was off limits until further notice. All events previously scheduled in the theater were now in the One Eighty Lounge. There would be no change in itinerary; we would spend the day at sea and dock in Santa Cruz de Tenerife tomorrow. She also informed us that the group of primarily men needed clothes or shoes, and donations could be dropped off at registration.

Harry and I walked downstairs to donate my bag of shoes and some of Harry's clothes, which were too big for him as he had dropped pounds while walking. I was pleasantly surprised to find a long line of passengers with arms loaded with clothes.

When I returned to my cabin, Suzette had left a phone message requesting I call her immediately, which I did. She needed my help as a translator and interviewer with the new guests, and I agreed to meet her at the starboard door of Stage Left. While putting on my personal protective equipment (PPE), jumpsuit, mask, and gloves, she filled me in on what she needed of me. They had prepared a questionnaire for each guest. Name, rank and serial number, what their belongings looked like, what they were fleeing from, and why. Suzette requested I start with the two women as I was female and not a crew member. She thought we were more likely to get the true story. She also asked that during my interviews, I gauge the tone, demeanor, and stress of these migrants and document that on the questionnaire.

As Suzette opened the door of the theater, I was assaulted by the smell of unwashed bodies, vomit, and feces. Suzette had told me that the refugees were "washed" and given jumpsuits before they were brought to Stage Left, so this was unexpected. It became clear to me that these people were in poor shape. They gorged on the food offered the night before, and being so hungry, it did not go down so well. Several crew members in PPE were doing everything they could to clean up. Two sitting areas, spaced far apart, with chairs and a table, were set up, and there was an officer and a refugee completing a questionnaire at each.

Suzette led me behind the stage curtain where the women were residing, and there was a table and chair off in a corner where I could work. I decided to interview the woman with the child first, as her son was sound asleep on a mat on the floor. I wanted to finish the interview before her son woke up. I gently ask this woman in French to follow me and have a seat at the table. She responded in French, and I brought her a cup of hot, sweet tea, hoping to relax her. Even in her emaciated condition, she was strikingly beautiful with long dark braids and a dark caramel complexion. She seemed frightened and avoided all eye contact with me. As she reached forward to pick up her teacup, I noticed handprint bruises on her upper arm, which were too large to be her son's.

We started with the basics: her name was Mariama, and her three-year-old son, named after his father, Mamando, was called Dou. She whispered to me that she left Senegal with her husband, Mamando, but he had passed away on the voyage. She started to cry. Thankfully, Suzette had left a box of tissues on the table. She told me her husband, a boat builder, lost his job since he broke his leg. There is no safety equipment or workman's compensation insurance. He had become unemployable, and if they were going to survive, they had no choice but to escape poverty and hunger. Mamando's cousin, Cheikh, owned a pirogue and made several trips a year to Tenerife, and he agreed to take them. They had no plan that she knew of once they arrived in the Canary Islands.

I then asked Miriama how her husband had died, and she got a terrified look in her eyes, refused to look at me, and, in a whisper, said, "He fell overboard while trying to land a big fish." I, being a poker player, am pretty good at detecting bluffs. I knew she was lying, but I did not pursue any more questions. I thanked her for her time and returned her to her mat.

I repeated my questions to the second woman, Awa, who indicated she was traveling with her husband, Cheikh, and was accompanying him to Tenerife to pick up supplies and return to Senegal. She seemed snobby like she was better than everyone. She acted like I was taking her away from something more important. She answered my questions directly, but I felt like I was not asking the right ones. I escorted her back to her mat and went around the curtain to the stage.

I caught Suzette's eye and she had me interview several men at one of the tables. All of them except one had a downtrodden demeanor and told the same story; they were headed to Senegal to find a better life when their pirogue encountered a storm, and they lost the engine. All the stories, but one sounded too similar. Malik, one of the healthier men, responded that he was traveling with his friend, Cheikh, and his wife, Awa. They were going to pick up supplies in Tenerife. Malik seemed shady to me; he was a follower, but he was covering something up.

Once all the initial interviews were complete, Suzette and I went to her office to compare notes. We agreed that getting close to Mariama was the key to getting to the truth. I suggested we isolate her and get her and her son secure in a cabin so we could chat more with her somewhere where she would feel safe and protected. So, Suzette and I devised a plan to have the medical staff inform the refugees that Dou had Covid19 and that he and Miriama were being isolated for everyone's protection. With no protests, we escorted Miriama and Dou to a cabin and locked them in for safety, as was done with all passengers who had come down with Covid19. I returned to my cabin for a long, hot shower. Suzette and I had planned to meet in her office at 9 am, where we would determine the next steps.

CHAPTER 34

Day Two After Rescue – Escape and A Few Answers

SOMETIME in the middle of the night, I was rudely awakened by the ship's alarm; my first thought was pirates! The clock told me it was a little after two am. The announcement directed the security crew and the Seals to go to the lifeboat stations on the starboard side of deck five. My cabin phone rang two minutes later. Harry told me to stay put and that he was getting dressed and going to check it out. I tried to talk him out of it, but he said he would not do anything stupid.

After what seemed like forever, Harry knocked on my door. I took one look at him and knew it was not good. I got a towel, wrapped up whatever ice was left in my ice bucket, and told him to put this on his eye. By dinnertime, he would have a black eye and a story to go with it. Once he had put the ice on his eye, he filled me in on the harrowing details. He said that two of the refugees, which I learned later were Cheikh and Malik, were caught trying to take a lifeboat from one of the secured lifeboat stations. He saw Tony and the First Mate, John, wrestling the two migrants to the ground. Tony had no trouble securing Malik, but Cheikh was too strong for John and had started the mechanics to lower a lifeboat and proceeded to climb aboard. Harry said he could not stop himself; he went to the lifeboat control station and stopped the boat from descending further. By then, John had recovered, grabbed Cheikh, and hauled him back to the deck. Harry and John were trying to subdue Cheikh when he hauled off and landed a punch to Harry's head, hitting him in the eye. Harry and John kept struggling with Cheikh until finally, Harry jumped on top of him, turned him over, and John got handcuffs on him. With the men secured, Tony took them down to the brig. He said that Gabe was still securing the door to Stage Left, so they would start an investigation later in the morning to determine how the two got out of the theater.

As soon as Judy recorded the daily briefing for the passengers, she and Tony met up with Gabe. It was time for Tony to relieve Gabe at the door. They also needed to determine how Cheikh and Malik escaped from the theater. It did not take long to find the unlocked catwalk door backstage, allowing Cheikh and Malik to find a way out. This exit was then secured, Gabe went to get a few hours of rest and Tony took over watching the door.

CHAPTER 35

Mariama's Story

AFTER a few hours of sleep, I met Suzette in her office, where we devised the planned for the day. She wanted me to spend all my time with Miriama in her cabin. I would bring lunch for all three of us, and when Dou went down for his nap, I would try to find out the truth about her ordeal. She also told me that the personal property of the refugees had been cleaned, and money and papers were sealed in plastic bags. Cheikh had over fifty thousand dollars in cash with him, re-enforcing the evidence against him as the boss of a human trafficking scheme. Malik had a few thousand dollars.

At 11:30 am, I had room service deliver soup, finger sandwiches, and chocolate pudding to Miriama's cabin, and I showed up a few minutes before them. As we ate, we chatted about her life in Senegal while her husband was working as a boat builder. Miriama's life was not easy, as she was solely responsible for Dou and the household.

They were lucky to have a single-family house leased from the boatyard owner, which was an easy twenty-minute walk to work for Mamando. He worked long hours, six days a week. Their house had no electricity, but it did have a small garden where Miriama grew vegetables. It was made of sundried clay bricks with a woven palm frond roof. Their house had an all-purpose room with pillows and cushions on a hard clay floor for sleeping and visiting. At night, the bed mats would be rolled out. This room had no windows. The house also had a kitchen with a stone hearth where Miriama cooked over an open flame. They ate and played games on a small, low table. Charcoal was used to cook and heat their home in the cooler weather, and it had to be carried from town every month or so. Though they had a well for water and an outside shared washroom between four houses, water for cooking and other needs had to be pumped and hauled to the house.

Every day, Miriama cooked breakfast of millet (a grain), which she would grind, add water, and boil, making hot "cereal." And every day, Miriama would walk a mile and back, carrying Dou to the port to buy fresh fish for dinner. She would pick vegetables from her garden and cook rice for their main meal in the early evenings. Once a week, she did the laundry by scrubbing it with soap on the rocks by the sea, carrying it home wet, rinsing it with fresh water, and hanging it on the line to dry. Sunday was the day of rest in their home, for Mamando, anyway. But he was a great husband and father, spending all his free time at home with his wife and son.

After lunch, I had room service pick up the dishes, Dou was put down for a nap, and Miriama and I sat out on the balcony so I could ask her the hard questions. I asked her to continue her story where we had left off. Cheikh agreed to take Miriama and Mamando to Tenerife. Cheikh said they were allowed to carry a small bag, bring a gallon of water each, a change of clothes, all their papers, and one small memento. She had taken a photograph of her wedding day, and Mamando had chosen a picture of all three of them, including her parents.

They met Cheikh at the pier close to the boatyard where he had the pirogue waiting. They loaded seventy-three people into a pirogue designed to hold forty. There were also three large bales securely wrapped in water-tight plastic. They were crammed together on the benches and on the floor between the benches. They would switch places every few hours so some could stretch out and others sat. They used their bags as backrests and pillows. Anything to try to make themselves feel comfortable. Everyone was instructed to use their water sparingly as it had to last them the entire journey. They were each given a slice of bread twice a day. Mamando offered Cheikh assistance wherever he could. He knew the other passengers had paid a significant amount for the opportunity, and Mamando felt obliged to do whatever he could to repay the debt.

The first two days were uneventful, and Cheikh kept telling them they were getting closer to Tenerife. However, Miriama noticed all the women, except Awa, Cheikh's wife, were constantly berated and manhandled by Cheikh and Malik. On day three, Mamando made his way to Cheikh at the back of the boat to help with bread distribution, and when Miriama turned back to look at him, he was gone, and there seemed to be some commotion. Miriama moved as quickly as she could to the stern, and she saw Mamando in the wake behind the pirogue, struggling for his life. And Cheikh looked on and was smiling. Miriama told me she was hysterical and tried over and over to get Cheikh to turn around and go back for him, but that he laughed at her and then slapped her. He grabbed her arm and told her to get back to her seat and stay there, and when they got back to Senegal, he was going to make her his second wife. He threatened her never to tell anyone what happened or he would kill Dou. Miriama had no choice but to go back to her son.

On day five, the gasoline for the boat ran out, and all they could do was drift at the mercy of King Neptune. Miriama said she was devastated about the loss of her husband and terrified of Cheikh, but she tried to do her best to hide her sadness from her son. Dou kept asking for his daddy and when he could go home, making the loss more devastating for Miriama. The water and bread were almost gone. Cheikh cut bread rations to one slice per day, and Miriama gave most of her share to her son.

The next two weeks went by painstakingly slow. Everyone was growing weak. Three had died of dehydration. Miriama had Mamando's water, so his death likely saved her and Dou's life. In the early morning of day twenty, the winds picked up, and the seas got rough, and as dawn broke, Miriama knew they were going to die. She hugged her son and prayed.

Before sunset, they spotted an oil tanker far in the distance, and Cheikh had two of the men try and row the craft in that direction; lucky for them, the currents were going straight at the tanker. If not, everyone would have perished. When Cheikh realized they would be rescued, he immediately threw the bales overboard. He and Malik then proceeded to throw the other women, all but Miriama and Awa, overboard. It happened so quickly, and everyone was stunned and had no time to react before it was over. Miriama shockingly understood that these women were to be sold in Tenerife as either house slaves or sex workers; she assumed that latter.

Miriama was stressed after spending two hours telling me her haunting tale. Dou had also started to stir from his nap, so I told Miriama to settle in for a quiet day with her son. I reiterated the fact that she was now safe. Cheikh and Malik were locked up, and they would never threaten or harm them again. And I would see her in the morning.

CHAPTER 36

Day Two After Dinner –
Even More Dreaded Mail

I HAD hoped we were done with mail. Harry and I were walking back from dinner to our respective cabins and saw mail at everyone's door. Harry came back with me so we could get the news together. The captain's letter stated that because of the refugees onboard, at least two of which had legal issues, Tenerife and the European Union would not let the Luna dock. Therefore, we would immediately start the seven-day transatlantic crossing to New York. We were both disappointed about missing Paris and London, but there was nothing to be done about it except to try to enjoy our last days at sea and contemplate that our epic journey was about to end.

The North Atlantic can be as rocky as the Pacific, so I had my Meclizine ready.

There was some exciting news in the letter. We would arrive at Pier 88 on the East River early on the fourth of July. Refugees would be processed by immigration authorities and assisted by the Red Cross. The NYPD would pick up Cheikh and Malik. Once this process was complete, the passengers were free to disembark to explore the city, returning to the Luna for a final dinner, after which we would have a front-row seat for one of the world's great fireworks displays. Harry and I thought this would be a fitting end to our voyage. We would say goodbye to Luna on July fifth and fly home.

CHAPTER 37

Day One of Transatlantic Crossing – Raven's Epiphany

HARRY and I met for breakfast, and I decided it was going to be my one and only sticky bun day. During the shortened 2022 world cruise, I found sticky buns on the third or fourth day. They were akin to the "Poppin' Fresh" variety but were drenched in honey and light as a feather, delicious. Since I knew these would put on the pounds, I ignored them when I saw them every day at breakfast.

As I sat down with my sticky bun and fresh fruit, I saw the captain and his officers enter the Cafe for their breakfast, and to my utter surprise and pleasure, spontaneous applause broke out. It was well deserved as these people risked their lives to save sixty-eight beings, sixty-six deserving, and protected all the passengers and crew. They were real heroes, in my view. It touched my heart to see this small gesture of gratitude.

After breakfast, I headed up to see Miriama and Dou, as I planned to do every morning until we reached New York. I felt connected to her and wanted to know more about her dreams and thoughts about going to America. When I knocked on her cabin door, she was showered, dressed, and ready for her day. She had finished breakfast, and Dou was absorbed in cartoons on the television. I ordered tea from room service, and we went out to the balcony to chat.

I broke the news about going to America as gently as I knew how, and she immediately broke down crying. As I got her some tissues, I asked her how she felt about this change. When she had gathered herself, I saw a smile on her face. She said they were tears of joy. Yes, she was terrified about going somewhere unknown, to a place where she did not know the language, but it was America. Everyone wants to go to America! I saw the excitement and terror in her eyes at the same time. It was at that moment that I decided I would help this young woman and her son as best I could to make her transition to her new home as smooth and less traumatic as possible. She had been through enough in her short life.

She told me she was twenty-two when she married Mamando and twenty-three when she had Dou. She had made it through high school and sat for the exams for admittance to higher education in Senegal, which is a difficult thing to do. Education is compulsory until the age of sixteen and free, but teacher and facility shortages and truancy are all issues. Miriama passed the exams, but there was no money for college. Miriama was needed at home to assist her mother in her hand-sewing business and supplement their income. Her father was a fisherman, and that is how she met Mamando.

Miriama said her dream was to work from home and have as much time with her son as possible. She loved sewing and dying fabrics in the bright colors of her African heritage. She said she had all the skills she needed and a head full of design ideas. I asked her to do some drawings today, and we could review them tomorrow. I suggested she and Dou watch some old Sesame Street episodes on the ship's TV system to get them started with English.

I left Miriama and told her I would see her in the morning, and I went off for a quick hot tub before my poker tournament. I saw Dexter when I arrived at the One Eighty Lounge at the makeshift poker corner. He pulled me aside and said he met Tony in the gym. He proceeded to tell me the "scoop" about the refugees, human traffickers, escape attempts, and probable drug connections. I feigned surprise and gave him my full attention while thinking, I was the one with firsthand knowledge. As requested by Suzette, I gave nothing away. Thank goodness I can keep a poker face. As the rest of the poker players sat at the table to play, I knew my goal was to have two thousand dollars in winnings when I left the ship. If I came in first, I would achieve that goal, but I had to beat Dexter. He and I had been trading wins. Usually, one of us would come in first, and one would come in second. I loved playing poker with Dexter, as I respected his game and thought he was a better player than I was, another reason I wanted to win.

As we all sat down to play, Inga was very animated; I could tell we would have no peace at the table. She started her gossip about the refugees quietly and then got louder. She said she heard that over ten people died from Covid19 on the boat, including three children. All the men onboard were part of a Senegalese gang that all had warrants against them for drug smuggling and had to escape quickly. That was why there wasn't enough food or water aboard the pirogue.

Dexter and I looked at each other. As I was sworn to secrecy, I said nothing, but Dexter knew the truth. He looked Inga in the eye and told her that the story was a lie, that she did not understand what she was talking about, and that the captain had requested we leave these people their dignity and privacy. He did not tell her the true story but warned her with a clenched jaw, "Stop gossiping." Dexter then took a deep breath and, in his usual calmness, looked at all of us and announced, "I made a one-thousand-dollar donation to assist the refugees in the name of all the poker players." I was moved by this generosity and went to the ladies' room to compose myself.

After my win, I pulled Dexter aside and told him what a wonderful and generous gift he had given these people. I had not heard that we could donate money, and he said Suzette had given him the okay. I asked if Dexter and his wife would join Harry and I for dinner. I would make reservations at Bistro Italiano. He was in. I found Suzette in her office, told her my plan, and asked permission for me to share that plan with Dexter, and she agreed. She also said she was on board, and if there was anything she could do to help, all I needed to do was ask. I made reservations for dinner and asked for a corner table by the window. I then left a message in Harry's room about dinner. I went back to the cabin to write up a Pros and Cons List and a To-Do List, as was a habit of mine from my days as a project manager. I then got ready for dinner.

Harry and I met up at One Eighty for a drink, which I needed. I quickly filled him in on my plan before the gang joined us. We all discussed our final dinner together and decided it should be in Prime Grille, and Gayle said he would take care of getting reservations. At

6:30 pm, Harry and I went upstairs to meet Dexter and Claudia in the restaurant. I was looking forward to the Zuppa di Fagioli Bianchi, white bean soup with Italian sausage, a specialty the chef lets cook extra-long so the soup is thick and rich with flavor. It was all I needed with a few baguettes. Yum!

After we all ordered dinner, I asked Dexter about his background. He told me he was a retired lawyer who played in high roller poker tournaments in Las Vegas and had played at the famous Aria's PokerGo Studio which is on my bucket list. I was in awe and jealous. I filled Dexter and Claudia in on what I had been up to and what I was planning. They immediately volunteered to help with the project. My first hurdle was to get Miriama's legal immigration issues resolved as soon as possible once we arrived in New York so she and Dou would not need to stay in detention very long. I had no contacts in the city nor knew of any immigration lawyers. Dexter had all the contacts and said, "he would handle it." Claudia also volunteered to work with Miriama and Dou on their English as she was a retired fourth-grade teacher.

I planned to visit Miriama and Dou every morning so I could work on their English as well. Claudia would see them every afternoon during the two-hour window when Dexter and I played poker. Talk about a crash course. We were all on the same page about finding a balance without overwhelming them. Claudia would put together lesson plans for both of us for the next few days. Harry suggested picking up sticky notes from the purser's office and naming all the objects around the room as a visual aid. It brought me back to my brainstorming sessions. It was invigorating. It felt like I was on a solid team of four, and we could make this happen.

As I was going to sponsor Miriama and Dou to get immigration status to the United States, Claudia and Dexter said they would like to share in rental expenses until Mariama got on her feet. I live in a tiny house, so living with me was not an option. I knew of a few new communities in my area with two-bedroom bungalows, which would be perfect for them to get started in, and since central Florida housing is reasonable, we all determined we could swing this. The public school system there would take Dou, and they had a robust adult education program for Mariama, whether English as a second language, how to open a small business or personal finance classes. A well-organized African community was nearby, run by a Christian church, which would support their transition and integration into life in America. Harry and I left dinner energized!

CHAPTER 38

Day Two of Transatlantic Crossing – Sharing

I KNOCKED on Miriama's cabin with my arms overflowing with children's books, games, and sticky notes. As I waited for Miriama to answer my knock, I heard singing in a beautiful soprano voice. When Miriama answered the door, she looked at me, and her face lit up with a huge smile. She invited me in, and she had our tea ritual ready. I dumped my offering on the couch, and we went out to the balcony. It was another glorious day, with sunshine and calm seas.

I first asked Miriama about her singing. She said she was a soloist at her church and had also been singing to Dou since he was a baby. We then both started talking at once and then we laughed. I started again and explained that I had a plan that I needed to share with her, so I requested to go first. I told her I wanted to sponsor her visa so she could stay in the United States and not wait an extended period before she could legally begin her life in her new country. Her mouth dropped, and then she started to cry. And then I began to cry. When she got her voice back, she asked why I would want to do this. How do you explain wanting to give back but never finding an outlet or opportunity? I said this was my opportunity. I explained that I felt a connection to her and her story and knew I could offer her the support she and her son would need to get started. She looked into my eyes, leaned over, and hugged me. I had to look away and get my emotions under control. At that moment, I knew I was making exactly the right decision.

I then went on to share the schooling plan and explained that we were waiting for a reply from a lawyer so that by the time we got to New York, many of the immigration hurdles would be crossed. I asked her if I could copy her documents and share them with the lawyer. She had no issue with that. Based on our discussion yesterday, I explained my plan once we were off the ship.

After our tea, we went back inside and saw that Dou had fallen asleep in front of the TV. Miriama put him in bed. I explained the books, games, and puzzles I had brought to keep them busy. I also took one of the sticky notes, wrote Television TV on it, and stuck it where it belonged. I told her Harry would be by to plaster her cabin with them and that Claudia would be by in the afternoon. I was going to keep her and her son busy. She laughed and was excited about the prospect.

She shyly smiled and asked if I was done with my news so she could tell me hers. I said yes, and then she smiled wide and started talking about her thoughts about the business she wanted to start and how she had many designs ready to go. Her base product was a white women's tee shirt that she would hand dye in Africa's iconic bright colors and then embellish with embroidery or beading in nature scenes. Her first design was bright green and purple with a beaded giraffe and acacia tree. I would be first in line to own it. She showed me several other designs, all of which were terrific. Her enthusiasm was contagious, and the concept was perfect for her and Dou's needs and could work well in the United States and, more specifically, in central Florida. I stood to leave, hugged her, and said I would see her in the morning.

During our afternoon poker tournament, Dexter caught me up on procuring an immigration lawyer. He told me his lawyer had connected to a partner in a local firm and directed him to one that specialized in immigration. Dexter had spoken with her and was impressed. He gave her all the details on Miriama's case, discussing the timeline and ways in which they might avoid detention for Miriama, specifically the timing on July fourth. She thought there could be an option to get a hearing before we arrived in New York by completing affidavits using the captain as an official witness to our statements. That sounded perfect, and I thought the captain would have no issues. I asked Dexter to contact the lawyer and get the details. After the poker game, I headed to Suzette's office to fill her in on my plan and requested she get permission from the captain.

Harry and I had made plans over two weeks ago to attend a dinner party for our trivia team, and I knew it would be great fun. I would have loved a peaceful hour and a hot tub, but there was no time. I settled for a hot shower and met Harry in the One Eighty for a much-needed drink. I filled him in on the day's events. He told me his sticky note exercise with Miriama went well. Harry does not speak French but does know Spanish, so they were able to communicate. Harry said Miriama was curious about me and had asked about Florida. Harry answered her questions as best he could with the language difficulties.

This was Harry's first meeting with Miriama, so I was interested in his reaction to her and whether he thought my plan was crazy. As I stated before, Harry does not like any conflict. I knew he might not tell me if he thought I was crazy, but after all our years as friends, I could read his body language. He shocked me by saying he was proud of what I was trying to do and would help however he could. He liked Miriama; he thought she was smart and funny, and he bonded with Dou.

We had a great dinner with the trivia team, and as usual, I skipped the show and crashed for the night. Dexter, Claudia, Harry, and I accomplished much in one day.

CHAPTER 39

Day Three of Transatlantic Crossing – Executing the Plan

IT was another beautiful day with calm seas. Thank goodness. If it had been rocky, I would not have been able to do everything needed. The first item on today's To-Do List was finding Dexter to see if he had gotten a response from the lawyer. Luckily, I met him and Claudia in the Cafe having breakfast. He told me the lawyer had provided all the details and the forms we would need. He suggested we go to the guest computer room, download the forms to my computer, and start filling them out. Claudia also filled me in on her afternoon working with Miriama. She said she was amazed at how quickly Miriama and Dou picked up English. She said they were progressing and mentioned that Harry had put sticky notes on everything. There were hundreds! She planned to work with them again in the afternoon.

As we all left breakfast, I used a house phone to call Miriama to let her know I would be late. Dexter and I stopped at my cabin to get my laptop; we downloaded the documents to my computer and printed a few copies to work from. Once that was accomplished, we headed to Suzette's office to fill her in on our progress and get the captain's response about being a witness. Suzette told us the captain had no issues, and we all looked over the affidavit forms. Nothing seemed out of the ordinary; we should be able to provide all the information needed.

Dexter and I parted ways, and I went up to Miriama's cabin with my laptop to start filling in the blanks. As I was let into the cabin, all I could do was laugh. There were sticky notes on every surface, walls, furniture, and fixtures. Harry had done a great job. His handwriting is also lovely and much better than mine. Job well done. My timing was good, as Dou was down for his nap.

I told Miriama that the lawyer said if she would testify against Cheikh and Malik, the judge would be more likely to grant her a visa. She was worried about her safety, but I reminded her they were going to jail for their crimes, and murderers got long sentences. She glanced over at her wedding and family pictures, and I saw the sadness take hold. She then squared her shoulders and agreed to testify against them.

I told her our goal for the day was to fill out the affidavit. She got her official papers and sat on the couch, and we started to fill in the blanks. When we completed her section, we chatted briefly about how she and Dou were doing and whether she had any questions or concerns. Her response was positive; she did not seem worried but excited about all these significant changes to her life we were planning. She showed me some more designs and asked for more drawing paper. We hugged each other goodbye, and I hurried back to my cabin.

I needed a hot tub and wanted a few minutes to myself. I quickly changed into my swimsuit, grabbed my laptop, and headed upstairs. There was no one there. My first order of business was a soak, which was heaven. As I stretched out on the double chaise to dry, I wrote the required essay on why I was willing to sponsor Miriama and why I had the means to support her. It did not take long as I wrote what was in my heart.

I had closed my eyes to take a nap when the cushion moved, startling me. Harry had come up to find me. He wanted to take pictures of areas of the ship that were our favorites, doing the things we did there so we could document our lives aboard the Luna. And, of course, my favorite place was exactly where I was. So, Harry took my picture as the first in a series.

I told him that I had seen Miriama and that he had done a fabulous job with the sticky notes. We made plans to meet up at One Eighty for afternoon tea.

Before the poker tournament, Dexter and I discussed the progress on the affidavit and I told him I had emailed him the form with both

Miriama's and my portions complete. Since Dexter was co-sponsoring them with me, he had to complete a section. He said he would complete it right after the game and email it to Suzette for her review with the captain. The goal was to have all sections completed and for all of us to meet in Miriama's cabin before dinner for the signing process. It appeared as if we were going to be able to complete this before dinner and send it back to the lawyer.

Harry and I rarely attended daily tea, as neither of us needed a fourth meal, but a few times on the journey, they had "Cupcake" tea with a large assortment of different kinds of cupcakes, which I love. They also have scones with clotted cream daily, another reason we tried to avoid it. Harry and I met as planned and studied the many tempting types of cupcakes. It was a hard choice. I knew I would have a scone after my cupcake, so I chose blueberry. To no surprise, Harry selected strawberry. His favorite birthday cake choices are pink (strawberry) cake or strawberry cheesecake. We both snapped pictures of tea.

Suzette was up at tea and informed us the captain would meet with us at 6 pm and we should meet her in her office ten minutes before then.

After thoroughly enjoying tea, Harry and I found all our favorite places around the ship and took each other's pictures doing our favorite things. We then went back to our cabins to prepare for dinner and our meeting with the captain and Suzette.

Harry, Dexter, and I met Suzette in her office, and she escorted us to the bridge. I had never done a bridge tour, and in the days of high security after 9/11, it was a rare privilege to be let into the inner sanctum. I did have a picture in my mind of how it would look: all floor-to-ceiling windows, a two-hundred-and-forty-degree view of the surroundings, an elevated captain's chair bolted to the floor with a handle for the ship throttle, a radar screen, and a GPS display. It was all that but brought into the twenty-first century. Many electronic consoles were spread out on either side of the captain's chair. They were for engine, stabilizer, and thruster control, communications, weather monitoring, and many more. Harry reminded me not to touch anything; he knows me well. My fingers itched to see what all those knobs and levers would do. As we left the bridge, we passed the manual navigation table with maps, a compass, and other navigational tools. Suzette told us it was staffed by one of the ship's officers, and his only assignment was maps. It was a cushy job in that he never had to take a watch.

The captain's office was off the bridge and was well appointed in traditional wood paneling and comfortable furniture. Suzette formally introduced Dexter, Harry, and me, and the captain motioned for us to take a seat around an inlaid wood table. She opened her laptop to the electronic signature application with the affidavit already loaded. Before we all reviewed the document, the captain asked us what made us decide to take on Miriama and her child and if we understood what this would mean to our lives at home. He said he respected the sentiment but wanted to ensure we understood the sacrifices. After we explained, he smiled and shook all our hands.

We each passed around the laptop, reviewed the statements, and electronically signed them. The captain was the last to sign and then offered congratulations. He passed each of us his business card and told us if we ever needed anything, we should reach out. As Suzette led us out through the bridge to the main corridor, she said she would get us paper copies and immediately forward the document to the lawyer so he would have it in plenty of time for the emergency immigration hearing scheduled for the morning.

Harry and I had a quiet dinner together, and we headed off to a show, which I had been looking forward to ever since Judy announced that Paulina and Charles were to perform their renowned cabaret show. Since the last set of entertainers could not get aboard due to the itinerary change, the host and hostess agreed to dust off and rewrite their show.

With Charles at the piano and Paulina at the microphone, they took to the stage in One Eighty. I never realized that Charles was a brilliant piano player. They had taken the words of their West End show and made them all about our journey around the world. Passengers and crew were singled out, events were highlighted, and Paulina, even with her British accent, made every word understandable. It was bawdy and hilarious like a cabaret show should be, but it was all about us. I was laughing so hard I got the hiccups and had tears running down my face. Each song in the act got better and funnier, and by the end, the audience, including myself, were on our feet applauding, as well as hooting and hollering. Every time I bumped into either of them around the ship, I was compelled to stop them and reiterate how much I loved their show. It was a fantastic way to end a momentous day.

CHAPTER 40

Day Four of Transatlantic Crossing

THE most crucial goal of the day was to hear back from the immigration lawyer concerning the outcome of the hearing. I knew I would be on pins and needles until I heard back. After meeting Harry for breakfast, I ordered tea to be sent to Miriama's cabin and went to meet her. She answered the door wearing a turquoise, purple, and pink Lily Pulitzer skort and matching tee shirt that fit her perfectly. I knew exactly who had donated these items as I had seen them on a passenger as she walked her two miles on the track every day. I love the prints Lily uses in her designs, and Miriama did the outfit justice.

Dou was singing the Sesame Street alphabet song in English as I walked through the cabin to the balcony, and all I could do was be amazed and smile. Miriama sat down for our tea, and I filled her in on all the events since I last talked to her, and she did the same. I asked if she wanted to try speaking only English with me from now on, and she heartily agreed. The conversation took longer than if we were speaking French, but we had the time. She said she would pray for the court to do the right thing, and I said as soon as I heard anything, I would let her know. I told her Claudia would come by in the afternoon.

I now had a day of leisure until the 2 pm poker tournament. Miriama's fate was out of my control, and even though I was on edge waiting to hear, I wanted to make the most of my free time on a sea day. It was another beautiful day, so I went to change and headed up to the hot tub, where I spent several blissful hours.

When I returned to the cabin to change, there was no news. I did not know if that was good or bad, but it was out of my control. Yuck! I went to the tournament a few minutes early to confer with Bobby, the casino manager, about the dinner I had planned with him as a treat for all five casino personnel. Three casino dealers were on the ship and rotated every twenty minutes when dealing, so the poker players got to know them all. They were skilled dealers, taking control of the action, and they were also pleasant and fun. I thought a dinner in a passenger dining room would be a nice change for them. When planning this, I conferred with Bobby and all the staff to determine their wants. It turns out that I had to climb through some hoops to make this happen. We had a ninety-minute window and could only go upstairs to the Cafe due to the limited time. I had to get permission from Bobby and Suzette. Bobby confirmed that everything was set and that the casino staff would meet all the poker players in the Cafe.

Dexter and I decided to call the tournament a draw since we had about the same number of chips, so we split the prize pool. I asked Dexter to check for news from the lawyer before I left for trivia, and he had not heard anything.

I told Harry he was on his own for dinner, but he knew where he could find me if he got any news about the lawyer. I went up for dinner with my bottles of champagne. Everyone seemed to have a good time, and all pulled me aside to thank me for my effort.

When I returned to my cabin for the night, Miriama's immigration status had not been updated.

CHAPTER 41

Last Day of Transatlantic Crossing

I T is our last sea day. I woke up and immediately thought about Miriama and Dou and if they would go home to Florida with Harry and me. There was still no word, and I was worried, as the hearing was yesterday. I did not want to see Miriama without news of her fate.

I turned on the TV, and the first thing I did was check the weather. I saw that it was another calm, sunny day. I donned my bathing suit and cover-up, called Harry to tell him I was going to breakfast, and headed upstairs. As I entered the dining room, Dexter and Claudia were waiting for me with the wonderful news. Mariama and Dou had visas to enter the United States, and Dexter and I were now financially responsible for them to be good citizens. Hurray! Harry joined us, and we all sat down for breakfast, relieved, and toasted our good fortune with mimosas.

After breakfast, Harry and I went down to Miriama's cabin to share the news. Harry had not visited for two days and was shocked when Miriama started speaking English! She said she had been practicing a lot. Harry went to Dou and distracted him while Miriama and I went to our spot on the balcony. She had a lot of questions about what to expect both at the Port of New York, and once we got to Florida. I let her know that Suzette and I would disembark the ship with her and Dou at 8 am with the other refugees. The immigration lawyer would meet us and handle whatever came after. Once the visa was issued, they would return to the ship with me, and she would go through the disembarkation process with me the next day.

When she returned to the ship, she had to organize her belongings, and I would bring her a backpack to put them in. When Claudia came by in the afternoon, she would pick up the games, books, and puzzles to return to the library. As I left, I said, "See you at 8 am." I gave her a big hug and left Harry playing with Dou. As I was leaving, it struck me that this was the end of the journey of a lifetime that I had worked so hard to achieve. It was surreal, sad, and amazing all at the same time.

The rest of my day was all about lasts. As I had no idea how long I would be in U.S. immigration with Miriama tomorrow, I went up for a soak in the hot tub. This is one place I will surely miss, as I do not have one at home. I wish I could take it with me.

I was then off to the last poker tournament, where we exchanged contact information and planned future SeaSpirit cruises. After the game, Dexter and I walked over to the coffee spot and got a cup of chai tea, a new favorite of mine. We took a seat and compared notes. I would be taking two thousand dollars in winnings home, and he would be taking home about the same, but he did give a very generous donation to the refugees, so he was clearly the winner of us winners. We both thought that none of the other players had made any money.

We also discussed tomorrow's logistics and my priorities for Miriama once we got home. Since I planned to play in the World Series of Poker Super Senior event next summer in Las Vegas, I would get to see him then. He told me that he and Claudia would visit Florida sometime in the winter. I would meet him tomorrow in Miriama's cabin at 8 am. We hugged goodbye, and I went off to play my last trivia game.

Our team earned many points, which enabled me to take home a lot of "S" logo merchandise, including hats, socks, key chains, cards, shirts, jackets, and backpacks. Miriama, Dou, and my friends are going to be walking advertisers for SeaSpirit.

I then went back to my cabin to pack. Ugh! And to change for the last supper with the gang of seven. I knew this would be emotional, but we all tried to keep it light and reminisced about our shared great experiences. There were lots of baguettes eaten, a lot of laughter, and there were a few tears, too. We all vowed to keep in touch.

After dinner, there was an event that SeaSpirit did once at the end of every world cruise: a crew auction. No, they do not auction off a crew member to take home, although Harry and I joked about doing just that. I would take the chef so I would never have to plan, shop, and cook again, and Harry thought his room steward would be helpful. I said, "Let's share them. You get them fifty percent of the time, so we never have to cook or clean again". We both chuckled and sighed, this was never going to happen.

This auction was a way to add money to the crew's emergency fund. We had been told about this a few days before and were asked to donate any items we would not take home. Harry and I both gladly donated as it was a great cause. I did not know what to expect. As we walked into One Eighty, Judy, the captain, several officers, Suzette, and all the entertainment staff were present. Suzette pulled me aside to advise that Harry and I should wait for her in Miriama's cabin in the morning, and she would pick us up at 8 am to escort us off the ship and take us to immigration.

The One Eighty was set up in a large semi-circle, with tables overflowing with stuff, including tee shirts, shoes, hats, closet organizers, wine; you name it, it was in the room somewhere. I had no idea how they were going to auction off everything in the two hours that were allotted, but they did keep to the timeline. We could examine the items around the room before the auction began.

Judy informed us that it was a speed auction. The first bid might be accepted immediately, or others might be allowed to counter bid. Once the high bidder was named, a staff member would bring the item(s) and complete the paperwork. She sternly told us, "Make your bid loud, clear, and quick by raising your hand high and speaking out." Paulina and Charles had come into the lounge, and they would be looking for the bidders. Paulina also acted as a model for jewelry and clothing.

I have never seen an auction like this. It was ridiculously fast. Judy and her team took similar or disparate items and put them in groups to auction off together. A grouping might include a bottle of wine, a pair of sneakers, and a feather boa. All of it was unexpected. Judy saved the best items for last, which were sentimental items the crew had donated. Judy even auctioned off the shirt on her back, which had been coveted by one of the passengers. They auctioned off the segment maps with Luna's exact course. They had a SeaSpirit triangular logo flag that flew for one hundred and eighty days on the bow with every crew member's signature. And my favorite was dinner with a crew member of your choice on the following night, the last night aboard.

The sale was a huge success, and they raised over five thousand dollars, which would be used to create a small outdoor space for the crew to enjoy during their limited free time. One of the dealers told me that she shared a cabin with another crew member, and the space was so small that they could not stand up simultaneously. The "lounge" area for the crew, where she went during her awake, non-working hours, was uncomfortable, and there was no outdoor space available.

As I retreated to my cabin for the night, I was overwhelmed. This incredible, once-in-a-lifetime experience was ending, and my life as I knew it would never be the same.

CHAPTER 42

New York, New York

HARRY and I got to Miriama's cabin a few minutes before 8 am, and Dexter was already there. We saw a Red Cross tent set up from the balcony and the NYPD standing by on the dock with two police cruisers. As we waited for Suzette, we saw two men being taken down the gangway by Gabe and Tony. The men were in handcuffs. Miriama pointed out Cheikh and Malik, who were handed off to the NYPD and each taken away in a cruiser. We never saw the other refugees disembark as Suzette arrived for us.

We disembarked through a terminal-connected gangway that ended in the large immigration and customs hall for Pier 88. I saw a man in a suit and tie off to the side with a sign that said Woodley, so I knew this had to be the lawyer. As our group approached him, he introduced himself, and we all shook hands. As Suzette took her leave, she wished us good luck and said she would see us back on board.

The lawyer said the immigration process should be simple, and he was correct. He took our small group to the booth in the center of the hall and explained to the officer that we had special circumstances and needed to see the officer in charge. The fellow spoke into his walkie-talkie, and a few minutes later, a woman in uniform approached. She introduced herself as the chief and led us to an interrogation room. It was intimidating, but she was friendly. The lawyer produced Miriama's and Dou's official visas; we all showed our passports. The officer then took us to an immigration booth, where a second officer scanned and stamped all the documents. It was official; we were official! The lawyer left us then, and since none of us had plans to go into the city, we were escorted back to the terminal gangway.

Miriama and Dou were now considered new passengers by SeaSpirit protocols, so they had their pictures taken and were issued identification cards that doubled as their cabin key. Once done, I explained that they could both wander around the ship and use the pool but warned that the other passengers might be curious and ask many questions. Miriama responded that she would rather go back to her cabin for the rest of the afternoon. I told her I would pick them up at 7 pm for dinner and that it would be something special.

As promised, Harry and I picked them up, and we went up to the Prime Grille and met Claudia and Dexter, who were waiting for us. When I called to make a reservation, I asked for a table in the back, a more private area. I did not want Miriama and Dou to be bothered by other passengers, who I am sure would have many questions. As we were seated, the maître d' brought Dou a booster chair and a coloring book to occupy him before our meal. I imagined they had not seen a child on board for a long time. The waiter came over with the champagne I had pre-ordered and popped the cork. Dexter proposed a toast "to new friends, new beginnings, and new adventures and success in all these endeavors." We click our glasses with a hearty "Cheers." We all started to put our glasses down when Miriama said she had a toast, which I translated into English. She said, "Thank you all. I have been blessed to have met you and pledged to make you proud." I, of course, got choked up but did my best to hide my emotions and click my glass all around.

As I helped Miriama order her and Dou's dinner, her eyes got as big as saucers. She said the only restaurant she had ever eaten in was the local outdoor food stall, where they cooked the traditional dish of fried pastries filled with meat, onions and spices served with tomato sauce. She and Mamando would go there on dates. As we were all chatting about our plans once we got home and waiting for the food to arrive, Inga spotted us and walked over to our table. She tried to be nice about being nosy but failed miserably. I was as evasive as possible and finally explained it was a private dinner for a reason. Some people will never change. When she left, I apologized to Miriama for her bad behavior.

Dou became quite excited when his burger and fries were delivered. It was clear he would have no trouble adapting to American food when we got to Florida. As usual, all the food was five-star, and we all enjoyed this last supper.

After dinner, with Dou asleep in Harry's arms, we all went up on deck to watch the famous Macy's Fireworks display. It is one of the most prominent displays in the world, with a row of barges strung in the center of the river. We were between two of them, so we could see the spectacle by looking in either direction. We could also hear the band playing the iconic patriotic songs of America. It seemed a perfect ending to my adventure of a lifetime.

CHAPTER 43

Disembarkation Day

WHEN I woke up, it hit me hard that this was the last day, and I would be in Florida in a few hours with two house guests. I watched Judy's final morning show, which included a surprising video. The captain presented over a thousand pounds of clothes, shoes, and sundries, as well as a check for thirty-five hundred dollars, to the head of the New York chapter of the Red Cross on behalf of Luna passengers and crew. The chapter president thanked him for the generous donation and said it would be used to support the transition of these refugees into American life.

Harry picked me up at my cabin, and we then picked up Miriama and Dou and headed to the gangway. Charles and Paulina were at the door, and we all got hugs. I introduced Miriama and Dou to them both, and they wished us safe travels. We walked down the gangway through customs and immigration and were on the bus for the transfer to the airport in no time.

EPILOGUE

A S I now reminisce about my wonderful experience, I cannot forget the poverty I saw in East and West Africa. The ruler of Dubai spent over sixty-two million dollars on an innovative, one-of-a-kind attraction, The Dubai Frame. Ten billion dollars was spent on advertising for the 2024 United States presidential election campaign. Think of all the good work this money could buy to find solutions to end such poverty. I am not a proponent of handouts, but I would rather see programs to train workers for living wage jobs and infrastructure projects like global wi-fi, bringing more jobs to a region. The average yearly income in Senegal is seventeen hundred dollars, barely enough to feed a family of two. The world can do better to lift these countries and citizens out of poverty.

On Thankfulness

I am overwhelmingly grateful for the opportunity of a lifetime. I worked extremely hard over long hours in a stressful job so I could earn this journey, and it was totally worth it. I am thankful and eternally grateful to have had this wonderful opportunity to fulfill my lifelong fantasy and to have done some good in the process.

I am thankful for my partner on this adventure, Harry. He kept me grounded and secure, distracted me, and calmed me down during stressful times. In a word, he kept me sane.

I am thankful to all (most anyway) of my fellow passengers for making the Luna my home away from home. We shared our lives and experiences and made lifelong friendships.

I am thankful to the officers of the Luna for keeping us safe in the storm and for risking their lives to save sixty-three human beings.

I am thankful to the ex-Navy Seals Gabe and Tony, who ensured the blackout curtains were closed every night and all anti-pirate protocols were followed. They also kept watch over all the refugees to keep us all safe.

I am thankful to the Luna crew for tirelessly trying to make us all happy. Whether the laundry staff hidden away in the bowels of the ship, the waitstaff trying to remember our preferences, or the cabin stewards cleaning our cabins, thank you all.

I am thankful for having the opportunity to meet Miriama and Dou and help them in their new lives. I know my life will be richer and more purposeful for it. I am thankful for the eye-opening, firsthand knowledge of human trafficking so I can lend my support to combat this widespread epidemic.

I have sailed around the world and visited over forty countries, sailed forty-five thousand and three hundred nautical miles (which equals about fifty-two thousand "regular" miles), visited about two dozen UNESCO World Heritage sites, and experienced places I have only seen in pictures and dreamed about, never thinking I would get the opportunity.

Never give up on your dreams; work as hard as possible to make them a reality. They can come true.

The End

ACKNOWLEDGMENTS

THIS book would not have been written without Craig Dorsey, my travel partner. We wrote a journal entry for each port of call so that Harry's father, who was no longer able to travel, could be part of our journey. These journals were my memories, and many of the details would have been lost without them.

Henry and Pamela Tom took a picture of the pirogue filled with refugees, and they generously shared their photograph for the cover of this novel. My deepest thanks.

Thank you to ChatGPT AI for assisting me with getting the facts right during my research.

Thank you to Carol Sue Revenel Deliere, who shared her own experience on self-publishing.

Thanks to my first readers, Janet Richards and Craig Dorsey, for their gentle honesty.

And finally, thanks to my friends and family for their support; you know who you are.

News Links:

Ialy - https://www.cruisehive.com/cruise-ship-encounters-tropical-storm-to-reach-kenya/134895

Rescue - https://www.youtube.com/watch?v=F4pOHq68Vpg

Printed in the United States
by Baker & Taylor Publisher Services